SIREN
Publishing

Men of the Bor

Ménage Everlasting

Loving Her Men

Marla Monroe

Men of the Border Lands 17

Loving Her Men

Nancy knows the dangers out in The Border Lands, but does she really need two men to keep her safe? Cayden believes she does and thinks that Mike is the perfect man to help him.

When Nancy and Cayden nearly die from exposure, Mike offers them a place to stay. He's wanted a woman to love and make the old house a home, but will Nancy agree to taking on two men? Cayden believes that the only way to keep Nancy safe is if he and Mike join forces to watch over her.

When spring finally arrives and they begin to put down roots, Nancy has to make a decision to either move on and find another house for her and Cayden or remain with Mike and turn his house into their home.

Genre: Futuristic, Ménage, Science Fiction

Length: 34,435 words

LOVING HER MEN

Men of the Border Lands 17

Marla Monroe

Siren Publishing, Inc.
www.SirenPublishing.com

A SIREN PUBLISHING BOOK

LOVING HER MEN

ISBN: 978-1-64243-376-0

First Publication: July 2018

Cover design by Les Byerley

PUBLISHER
Siren Publishing, Inc.
www.SirenPublishing.com

ABOUT THE AUTHOR

Marla Monroe has been writing professionally for over thirteen years. Her first book with Siren was published in January of 2011, and she now has over 85 books available with them. She loves to write and spends every spare minute either at the keyboard or reading. She writes everything from sizzling-hot cowboys, emotionally charged BDSM, and dangerously addictive shifters, to science fiction ménages with the occasional badass biker thrown in for good measure.

Marla lives in the southern US and works full-time at a busy hospital. When not writing, she loves to travel, spend time with her feline muses, and read. Although she misses her cross-stitch and putting together puzzles, she is much happier writing fantasy worlds where she can make everyone's dreams come true. She's always eager to try something new and thoroughly enjoys the research she does for her books. She loves to hear from readers about what they are looking for in their reading adventures.

You can reach Marla at themarlamonroe@yahoo.com, or
Visit her website at www.marlamonroe.com
Her blog: www.themarlamonroe.blogspot.com
Twitter: @MarlaMonroe1
Facebook: www.facebook.com/marla.monroe.7
Google+: https://plus.google.com/u/0/+marlamonroe7/posts
Goodreads:
https://www.goodreads.com/author/show/4562866.Marla_Monroe
Pinterest: http://www.pinterest.com/marlamonroe/
BookStrand: http://bit.ly/MzcA6I
Amazon page: http://amzn.to/1euRooO

For all titles by Marla Monroe, please visit
www.bookstrand.com/marla-monroe

TABLE OF CONTENTS

LOVING HER MEN

Men of the Border Lands 17

MARLA MONROE

Chapter One

Mike climbed the steps to his front porch and let out a long breath. Damn, it was good to be home again. He'd thoroughly enjoyed the Thanksgiving meal his sister, Kate, and her two husbands had prepared, but the long walk back had worn him out. It had been over a year since he'd recovered from the gunshot wound when some men had tried to steal his sister away. He'd been extremely lucky not to have succumbed to the wound when infection had set in. Even now, he sometimes felt a pain in his chest from it.

He grabbed a couple of logs and threw them in the fireplace to build up the dying embers. It was cold outside and the scent of snow was already in the air. He had little doubt it would snow before the end of the week. He was thankful that the guys had helped him cut plenty of firewood for the winter and had shared their garden results, as well. He'd been in no shape to maintain a large one himself. Even now, he struggled some days. That would all change come spring. He'd be well enough to tend his own garden and cut his own wood.

Stupid, wallowing in the past. I'm alive and able to take care of myself now. That's a lot to be thankful for.

Still. Mike felt completely isolated now that Kate had a family of her own. With her being pregnant again, the guys looked like peacocks strutting around the house, and who could blame them? He was happy for her and them, but it drove home the fact that he was alone there and despite how close they were, he didn't see them as often as he'd like. Little Jay was nearly five months old now. He looked just like Kate and reminded him of her as a child.

Once he had the fire going strong, Mike opened the pack he'd carried back and deposited the food they'd sent home with him in the fridge. As cold as the house was other than in the living room where the fire was, it would be fine until he warmed it for dinner the next day. How she'd managed to create the feast she had, Mike had no idea. It had been delicious and reminded him of home once again.

They'd talked about their respective homes over the meal and how much they missed the people from before. They'd had some laughs and a few tears, but it had been a good time, to say the least.

If only I had someone to spend the long days and nights with here, maybe I wouldn't miss everyone so much.

Then again, wishing for anything in the current environment was useless. Women were at a premium in the Border Lands. In fact, they were a commodity that was bought and sold like a horse or cow. It disgusted him that he'd had to draw up papers on his sister and sign them over to Bruce and Marcus so that some bounty hunter didn't try to take her away from them.

Kate was lucky in that they had been smart enough to start putting solar panels up as they found them. She'd have electricity before long. That would make life for her so much better. The guys had offered to add some to his house, but he'd said not until they had their own house completed. He didn't need them anytime soon. Living like he did when it was just him didn't bother him so much.

I've got to get out of this funk I'm in. This isn't like me to wallow in self-pity.

He blamed it on the holiday, and the fact that he was coming up on being another year older. Time seemed to be slipping past him at a faster rate these days. A year had changed a lot in his life. He'd cut himself some slack and ride out the darkness dwelling inside of him. It would start to lift once winter was over. At least that's what he told himself.

Mike carried in enough wood for the rest of the night and into the next day. Then he climbed on the couch and bundled up in front of the fire. He needed to clean up and get ready for bed, but it was just too easy to remain like he was and for now, he wanted to enjoy being alive to see his future niece or nephew born.

* * * *

Nancy struggled to put one foot in front of the other. The snow wasn't that deep, but her body was that tired. She and Cayden had been walking for the last two hours and her body begged for a break, but her head knew they couldn't stop until they found shelter. They'd never have left the last one knowing winter was coming had it not been for the attack from the two men trying to take her from Cayden.

Cayden had managed to kill one of them, but the other one had gotten away. They had no idea if he'd been injured enough that he couldn't follow them or not. They weren't taking any chances.

The sky looked heavy, as if it would drop another load of the soft cold stuff on their head at any minute. Nancy prayed they'd find somewhere to stay before then, or they'd freeze to death out in the elements. The only shelter they'd had so far had been a shallow cave that had offered little in the way of comfort. It smelled of animal musk, and Cayden had been worried whatever had been in there might return at some point.

So, there they were, walking in the ankle deep snow and praying for a place to hole up until winter had passed.

That's at least four months, if not longer. We could starve by then, and all of this would have been for nothing.

Nancy trudged on, following Cayden's steps as best she could. Twice she fell after stepping on a stick she hadn't seen in the snow.

Cayden continued on, without knowing she'd fallen. For a quick instant, she considered just staying down. He'd have a better chance without her, but that was cruel to him. He'd blame himself if he lost her.

She cared for him more than she'd ever cared for another man. They'd been together for nearly a year now and the bond between them had slowly grown deeper over time. It was just too bad that they'd had to leave their last home. They'd carved out a decent life for themselves there, but traveling deeper into the Border Lands was their only chance at being together. There were fewer and fewer of the bounty hunters out there with all the families banding together to keep them away. Nancy hoped they could find one of the groups they'd heard about from travelers about the Border Lands. They were their best chance at survival as a couple.

"Nancy, are you holding up okay?" Cayden stopped and turned to look at her.

"I'm fine. Getting tired, but I can go another mile, I think. Just until we find somewhere safe to rest."

He sighed. "I'll find us somewhere. Just don't get behind so that I lose you."

"I'm keeping up."

He took a step toward her and pulled her into his arms. Despite the coldness of the outside of his coat, his arms were warm to her, fueled by his love for her. They hadn't said the words to each other, but she knew they both cared more deeply than how friends did. They'd been intimate since spring when she'd left the commune with him to find their own way in life. She'd never looked back, preferring Cayden over the odd rules and expectations there.

They'd been doing fine until the men had come and tried to steal her away from Cayden. She'd thought she'd recognized the one that had gotten away as one of the men from where they'd left but hadn't mentioned it to Cayden. It was something she could believe of them, but Cayden wouldn't have wanted to believe that any of the men he'd called friend would have stooped so low.

"Hopefully we'll find an abandoned house soon. I'm worried that it's going to start to snow again come nightfall," Cayden told her.

"We'll be fine."

"I know."

She sighed and picked up one foot to put in front of the other as Cayden strode forward. Thoughts of how he'd made love to her that last night before the men had attacked warmed her as she followed her man. He'd been tender and caring that time. Sometimes their coming together had been wild with the adrenaline of hard work and the slow burn of teasing they'd done. But every time, Cayden had made sure she'd climaxed before he'd come himself. She couldn't ask for a better lover.

"Looks like a house of some kind ahead. Wait behind these bushes while I check it out. I'll come back and get you if it's empty and looks sound enough to hole up in for a few days."

Nancy crouched behind the bushes, sitting on an overturned log, and hugged herself to keep warm. Cayden was gone long enough she started to get worried. Finally he returned with a huge grin.

"Looks like it's empty, but someone has it set up like a half-way house." He helped her up.

A half-way house was one used when a trip took two days and they kept a structure set up for when they needed to bed down for the night. That meant there'd be food, blankets, and wood for a fire. They couldn't have gotten any luckier.

She walked hand in hand with Cayden and climbed up on the porch fraught with loose boards. She sure hoped it was in better shape inside. When Cayden opened the door it was to a crackling fire and real heat for the first time in more hours than she could count. Nancy immediately walked over to stand in front of the roaring fire, pulling off her gloves to hold her hands out in front of her.

"Good, huh?" Cayden removed both his gloves and his coat, unwrapping the scarf from his neck. He draped all of it over one of the chairs.

"Perfect. It feels good to be warm again."

"Take off that coat so you can get warm faster."

He helped her pull it off and draped it over another chair with her scarf and gloves, as well. She smiled up at him and sighed at their good fortune.

"Hey, this is perfect," Cayden said. "We've got a lot to be thankful for and it's Thanksgiving today."

"I'd forgotten. It's been hard to keep up with the dates," she said.

"I may have it off a day or two, but today we have this to be thankful for, so I say it's Thanksgiving. Wait here while I find something to eat. Anything will be better than deer jerky."

Cayden gave her a warm hug before lighting a candle and carrying it into what she supposed was the kitchen at the other end of the living room. She smiled to herself. He was right. They had plenty to be thankful for even if it wasn't exactly Thanksgiving.

A few minutes later Cayden returned, carrying a cast iron skillet, a cast iron pot with meat inside and two plates with silverware balanced on top. His face held a huge grin as he set it all down on the hearth.

"What's all that?" she asked.

"Food. Whoever keeps this place up had a cooler in the kitchen with frozen meat in it. I also found some canned beans in the pantry. Looks fresh from a garden. Wish we could thank them, but the most we'll be able to do is put it back to rights before we leave."

"What kind of meat is it?"

"Looks to be rabbit. Too large for squirrel and too small to be much else."

"Whatever it is, I'm excited."

Nancy helped him by pouring the canned beans into the pot and setting it to one side of the fire while he settled the supposed rabbit into the skillet with water and what looked like chopped onions. He sat the skillet on the edge of the fire, stirring it periodically, so the meat wouldn't stick to the bottom of the pan.

It wasn't long until the room smelled of the slowly roasting meat and green beans. She stirred the beans and pulled them farther from the fire when they started boiling. They'd need to add more water so that they wouldn't boil dry.

"Is there running water or will we have to melt some snow?" she asked.

"Melt some snow. I got a big pot full of it earlier. It might already have melted some. I need it for the rabbit. I'll bring back enough for the beans, as well." He stood and made his way back to the kitchen.

An hour later they feasted on rabbit with light gravy and beans. Nancy couldn't remember the last time they'd eaten that good. Well, maybe she could. They'd had squirrel with potatoes and onions the night before the attack. Still, it had been nearly a week since they'd been walking and it was a meal to be thankful for indeed.

"We'll sleep down here on the couch. The fire will keep us warmer than sleeping in one of the bedrooms," Cayden said.

"I agree, but I don't think we'll both fit on the couch," she said with a smile.

"You can either sleep on top of me or we can sleep feet to feet as long as you promise not to kick me in the balls."

"My legs are short enough I don't think I'll be able to reach that far north."

Cayden smiled. "Let's clean up the dishes then get settled in. I want to enjoy as much of this as possible before we need to get going again. If it snows tonight, we might be here for a few days, but if it doesn't, I'd really rather get back out there to look for a place that doesn't belong to someone else."

As soon as she'd finished her meal, Nancy helped Cayden clean up everything then waited until he'd added wood to the fire before climbing on the couch and settling herself with a fluffy pillow on one end while Cayden took the opposite end. She was right, her feet didn't quite make it to the danger point for poor Cayden. Still, she made sure she kept her feet on the outside of his legs and turned toward the fireplace and the delicious heat it put out.

"Do you think we'll find somewhere to live soon?" she finally asked.

"I hope so. There have to be more houses out here like this. Even if it's not in the best of shape, as long as the structure is sturdy, we can work on it. It just has to get us through the winter, hon. We can take care of any issues it has come spring."

"What are we going to do for food? Everything around here's probably been scavenged. Besides, most of the canned goods have gone out of date and are ruined. It's been over eight years since all the disasters tore everything apart."

She still couldn't get her head around how so much had happened in such a short amount of time. She'd thought it was the end times from the Bible. There'd been floods, earthquakes, fires, tornadoes, and even tsunamis that had devastated every area of the United States and Canada. As far as she knew, it had happened all over the world. All she knew was that she'd been barely sixteen and after losing everyone in her family had traveled with her friends to where they'd found a little commune that offered safety in numbers and a way to survive.

Nancy had met Cayden when he'd arrived at their camp roughly four years ago and had known almost instantly that she liked him. It wasn't until she'd turned twenty-three that they'd agreed to cohabitate in the commune. Then, when the rules and beliefs of some of the leaders had become more than either of them were willing to live with, they'd struck out on their own, finding a small farm about three days away, making it their own.

"You warm enough, hon?" Cayden asked a few minutes later.

"Mmhmm. Toasty. What about you?"

"Good and warm. Just wish we could hold each other instead of sleeping like this, but I have a feeling if we'd tried to sleep with you on top, one of us might have ended up on the floor in the middle of the night."

Nancy giggled. "I think you're right. Besides, you'd snore in my ear."

"I don't snore."

"Do too."

"Night, hon."

Chapter Two

Mike carried in more firewood as the first fat flakes of snow began to fall. He'd made three trips already, but needed to make another two or three to be sure there was enough wood sheltered on the back porch, as well. Once this storm got finished, he was fairly sure he'd be snowed in for a good three or four days.

He'd visited with his sister and her family the day before, knowing they'd all be confined to their homes for the duration of the storm. She'd been doing well, and her men were doting on her as if she were a china doll. Mike was thankful he'd chosen them for his sister every time he was around them. Had he picked one of the younger groups of men, he didn't think she would have been nearly as happy, and certainly wouldn't have thrived as she had.

I can't wait for the baby to be born. I just pray that they're both healthy.

He finished loading the back porch with wood then checked to be sure the cooler was still locked up tight. Raccoons were notorious at opening things to get at any food they thought might be inside of something. He'd caught several trying to fiddle with the lock he had fixed up on the two coolers he kept on the back porch with whatever he'd managed to catch or kill inside them.

Tonight he had a slice of deer steak thawing in the sink to fry up on the fire. Mike wasn't going to bother with vegetables tonight. He just didn't feel like the extra effort. Cutting and stacking wood the last two days had worn him completely out.

The snow had picked up by the time he'd walked inside. He had no doubt it would turn into a full-blown blizzard before the night was over. He was lucky to have a roof over his head and food to eat. He felt sorry for any poor sap out in the snow. Hopefully they'd find shelter before they froze to death.

One of the things the guys had suggested was that putting solar panels on his roof would also mean they could hook up walkie-talkies or short-range radios, so that they could talk to one another since their houses weren't really that far away. Some of the nicer units reached more than forty miles. With his sister pregnant, Mike thought that a good idea. That way if they needed him they could contact Mike without one of the men having to come get him. He was leaning more and more toward getting set up with the solar panels every day.

The trick was finding enough of them in the area to work. They'd need a way to locate them close enough that it wasn't dangerous to leave his sister behind, and a way to transport them once they found them. They'd have to talk more once the worst of the cold weather was behind them, but before they needed to start breaking ground on their gardens.

I'd like to be able to talk to her sometimes just to know that she's happy and the guys are being good to her.

Mike missed having her around. It got lonely there in the house by himself. It was a rather large place for just him. If there'd been a smaller place close by, he might have considered moving, but there wasn't. He'd looked. He had a half-way house about ten miles off between his place and the nearest town they tended to scavenge from. That was too far to live from his sister though.

He fried up the deer steak and ate, listening to the blowing wind outside and the crackling of the fire. It felt good to be warm after having been out in the cold air most of the day. He'd sleep on the couch again instead of in the cold bed upstairs. Mike had a feeling he'd be sleeping on the couch most nights that winter. It was just too cold to sleep in one of the beds upstairs by himself. Now if he'd had a woman…

I've got to stop dwelling on being alone. This is just the way it's going to be.

The soft whine of something outside his front door had him grabbing the ax he kept by the fireplace when he was inside. It sounded like a wolf. Why would one be whining at his front door?

Another whine then a yelp with a scratch at his door clued him in that it was more than likely a dog and not a wolf. Still, most of the dogs that had survived were wild and ran in packs much like the wolves.

He looked out the window to the right of the door and found what looked like a Newfoundland scratching with both feet at his door.

"What the fuck?"

Mike unlocked the door, keeping the ax ready in case the thing attacked him and opened the door an inch. The dog barked then whined again. He opened it more and the dog rushed in then turned around and rushed back to Mike. He sat and gave a little yip before prancing toward the door once more.

"What do you want? I'm not playing in and out with you. Either you want inside for the night or you want out. Can't say I know why you'd want back out in that, though."

The dog walked up and gently grabbed Mike's shirtsleeve and tugged at him as if he wanted him to follow him outside.

"No fucking way, boy. I'm not going out in that for any reason. You can go out, but I'm staying right here where it's warm."

The dog sat next to the door, whining. Mike sighed and opened the door to let it out, but it grabbed his shirt sleeve again and growled as he attempted to pull Mike outside with him.

That's when it hit him. A dog this friendly had to belong to someone. That meant that someone might be close by and in trouble. The dog was trying to get whoever it was some help.

"Okay, boy. I get it. Let me get my coat, or we'll all be in trouble." He jogged into the kitchen and grabbed his coat, scarf, and gloves, throwing them on as he hurried back to where the dog stood at the closed door prancing as if urging him to hurry up.

"Let's go. Show me where your owner is."

Mike followed the dog as it raced forward then turned back to let Mike catch up with him. They slowly made progress through the blowing snow until Mike wasn't sure where they were. He prayed the dog could find his way back to his place once they located whoever was out in the woods. He wasn't sure he'd be able to.

Finally, the dog disappeared not far away inside a grouping of rocks. Mike walked toward it as fast as he was able then ducked inside where he found not one, but two people wrapped up in each other's arms, covered with snow.

"Holy shit."

They looked as if they were frozen solid, but when he reached over to check the pulse at one of their throats, he found it thready, but there. He checked the other one and found the same thing. They were alive, but unless he could coax them up and get them moving again, he'd lose them for sure. He couldn't carry both of them. Hell, he wasn't sure he could carry even one of them.

"Hey, wake up." He shoved the snow off them and began punching at them to stir them up.

Neither of them seemed to respond at first, but the more the dog licked at their faces and he shook them, they started to rouse.

"W—what?" a weak masculine voice croaked out.

"Wake the hell up. You're going to die if we don't get you back to my place soon." Mike pulled on the man, realizing that the other one was a woman. "Do you want the woman to die?"

"Take her. Get her warm. You can see about me later," the man managed to get out.

"I'm not leaving either one of you. Get your ass up." Mike punched him hard in the arm.

The dog grabbed the man's other arm and began tugging on it, letting his teeth nip into his skin. The man yelped but slowly pulled himself up using the rock behind him. He tried to tug the woman up, as well, but he didn't have the strength. Mike pulled her up and shook her.

"Wake up, lady. You need to help your man before you both die here. Wake up," Mike said, shaking her hard enough he was worried he'd break her fool neck as her head wobbled.

Finally she groaned and opened her eyes. They were the prettiest brown he'd ever seen. They reminded him of milk chocolate. Right now, though, they were hazy with sleep. She allowed him to pull her to her feet then clung to the man as the dog stood on the man's other side.

"We're going to walk out of here and to my house. It's not too far, but you've got to keep moving. I can't hold you both up. Got it?" he yelled.

"Yeah. Keep moving," the man croaked out.

"Good. Let's go." Mike kept one arm around the woman's waist throwing her arm over his shoulders as he maneuvered them through the rock's opening and around to the outside.

It took much longer to reach the house than it had to follow the dog out to where they'd been. Several times the man had faltered, but Mike's rough voice and the dog's insistent barking had him going once more. Mike knew it was sheer will that had the stranger putting one leg in front of the other one with the help of the dog's nips and barks.

Mike had to all but drag the poor woman as she stumbled over her own feet as well as anything in her way. He was worried that she'd die before they managed to get to the house, but she seemed just as determined as her man to make it all the way. Once they got there, Mike was at a loss as to what to do with them to warm them up. The bed would mean climbing stairs and that wasn't going to happen in the shape there were in. His only option was to make a warm pallet in from of the fireplace and warm them up there.

As soon as they were inside, Mike sat them on the floor directly in front of the fire then raced up the stairs to grab every blanket and covering he could carry. Then he made a second trip up for pillows. When he returned to make out the makeshift bed it was to find them fast asleep in each other's arms with the dog half on, half off of their lower halves.

Damn, that dog was loyal. He couldn't imagine how they'd managed to train it to get help in the sort of wild and dangerous world they lived in. He urged them out of the way and folded out the various blankets then pulled the top three up and started undressing them, urging them to help.

"Too cold." The woman's teeth chattered as she tried to talk.

"You'll warm up faster without these wet, freezing clothes on," Mike told her.

"Do it, Nancy. He's right." The man's voice was just about gone.

Mike bet he'd been coaxing the woman for a long time for it to be so raspy and weak. He would have kept her going by goading her then demanding it until she finally fell and didn't get back up. What in the hell were they doing out in the storm in the first place? Why would they have ever risked walking when there was a chance they'd have a storm come through? He had no idea, but if they didn't die, he'd find out.

* * * *

Nancy didn't want to wake up. In her dream she was toasty warm and comfortable. Cayden was on one side of her, and…and who was on the other side of her? Her eyes flew open even as her body stiffened beneath the covers.

"Easy, Nancy. You're safe. Your man is right there on the other side of you. I'm just helping to keep you both warm." The man's voice was soothing, though a little rough. "How do you feel?"

"I—I'm okay. Who are you? How did we end up here?" she asked as she looked over at Cayden, relieved that he actually was on the other side of her.

If he was there with her then everything would be fine. She believed he would always take care of her.

"I'm Mike. This is my place. Your dog came and got me for you. He must have smelled the smoke from my fire and figured I'd be able to help. You've got a good dog there," the man said.

"Dog? We don't have a dog." Nancy was confused.

"That's not your dog on the other side of your man?" Mike asked.

Nancy lifted up just enough to look over at Cayden and see the huge furry dog lying next to him. She'd never seen the dog before, but it looked friendly enough.

"We don't have a dog. I don't know where it came from," she said, looking over at Mike for the first time.

The man's hazel eyes shown with obvious compassion as she stared into them less than a foot away. He had sandy, light brown hair that needed a cut even for being shaggy.

"Well, looks like you have one now. He seems like he's adopted you. You'd be dead without him coming to find me. I don't know how he found you unless you stumbled into his resting place."

"Is Cayden okay? He hasn't woken up," she said, changing the subject.

"He's exhausted, I'm sure. Let him rest. Your name is Nancy, right?" he asked.

"Yes. Cayden and I were trying to find a safe place to hold up through winter, but got caught before we could. I wish we'd stayed back at the half -house we'd found. We'd have been okay there."

"That's my place. Why didn't you?" he asked.

"We weren't sure if you'd find us and be angry that we'd used it. We cleaned up after ourselves. I promise we didn't hurt anything." Nancy realized she was lying right next to him and he might not be happy that they'd used his place.

"I'm sure you didn't. You should have stayed there where there was food and shelter. Why were you traveling in the first place? You had to know with winter coming on it wasn't safe," he said.

"Nancy?" Cayden turned toward her, then gasped. "Who the hell are you?"

"I'm Mike. I pulled you in out of the snow," he said.

"Are you okay, Nancy?" Cayden asked her. She snuggled back into Cayden's arms.

"I'm fine. He was telling me that we should have stayed back at the half-way house. It was his," she told him.

"I wish we had. If I'd have known you wouldn't have been mad and found us there, we would have tried to wait out the winter there. I never expected it to turn so cold so quick," Cayden said.

"What in the hell were you doing wandering around out here so close to winter in the first place?" Mike asked.

"The place we were staying wasn't safe for Nancy anymore. I wasn't about to let her be tossed around from one man to the next. It's one thing to share a woman with another man and another to have her move around between households just so every man in the damn place can have one," Cayden said.

"Where was that?" Mike asked. He'd sat up, the blanket pooling in his lap to reveal that he was bare-chested.

Nancy was pretty sure from what she could remember from when she'd first woken up he was bare below, as well. She knew Cayden was naked except for his underwear. She only had on her panties. She should have been shocked, but considering how warm she was and how cold she remembered being, she wasn't going to complain.

"We were living in a commune back near old St. Louis. The first few years weren't bad. We all worked together and shared what we grew. There was cattle, chickens, pigs and plenty of fresh vegetables. Then the older men died out and the younger ones started making rule changes. Stupid changes at first. Then came the one where since there were so few women, it was best if they were shared between several men. Not two or three, but six and seven. They'd spend time with a few here then move on to the next group after a few weeks." Cayden shook his head. "It made me sick to think of Nancy shared like that."

"I don't blame you, but you should have found a place and laid low through the winter," Mike said.

"That was the plan and we did. Had a nice place we planned to homestead, but, I don't know, four or so weeks ago two men attacked us and tried to take Nancy. We had to leave before the one I didn't kill came back." Cayden looked over at her. "I think they were from our old commune. I recognized one of the men."

Nancy sighed. She should have known Cayden wouldn't have missed anything. They were both young with her only being twenty-five to Cayden's twenty-six, but he was smart and kind. She'd fallen for him almost from the beginning. If not for him, she'd have ended up shared with nearly a dozen men. The thought made her stomach roll like a tumultuous wave in the ocean.

"Don't guess you had much choice then. I can understand the need to keep moving. It's all behind you now. You're here and are welcome to spend the winter with me. If I don't have enough for all of us, my sister and her men are about an hour's walking distance. Maybe a little more in the snow." Mike scooted out of the covers and stood up, wearing only a pair of boxers.

Nancy gasped at the sight of his shirtless body and quickly turned into Cayden's arms. He was tall, though not as tall as Cayden, and had a large scar on his upper chest that looked as if he'd been shot. Maybe he had. His wide chest and muscular arms spoke of hard work, but he was also lean like Cayden though she knew the reason behind Cayden's. They'd been hungry for a long time now.

As if thinking about it, her stomach picked that moment to growl like an angry momma bear. She groaned as both men laughed.

"I've got food to warm up. Your clothes should be dry by now if you want to get dressed. Are either of you having trouble breathing? I don't want you to end up with pneumonia from being half frozen in the snow." Mike's voice sounded as if he'd walked farther across the room.

"I'm okay. What about you, Nancy?" Cayden asked, pulling her face out of his shoulder.

"I'm okay. My throat hurts, but it's not bad. I probably just need something to drink," she said.

"Get dressed, and I'll bring you something to drink," Mike said.

The second the other man had left the room, Nancy jumped up and pulled on her clothes. She was still cold, so she wrapped one of the blankets around her and sat next to the fire while Cayden finished dressing.

"Are you really okay, Cayden?" she asked.

"Yeah. I'm good. He didn't hurt you, did he?" Cayden asked, kneeling in front of her.

"No. He didn't. I guess we owe him and that dog our lives. They saved us," she told him.

"His dog is pretty damn big. Seems nice enough."

"It's not his dog, Cayden. He thought it was our dog since he came and got Mike to rescue us. The dog led him right to where we were. I can't even remember anything before when it first started snowing. We're lucky the dog found us and alerted Mike," she said.

"Well, thanks, dog. Whatever your name is." Cayden scratched the huge animal between the ears. It earned him a massive tail wag and a sloppy wet tongue across his hand.

"Eww," Nancy said with a grin. Then she sneezed three times in a row.

"Damn. I hope you aren't getting sick, honey." Cayden sat down next to her and pulled her back into his arms.

"I'm just cold. I'll be better once I warm back up."

Nancy wasn't so sure about that. Her chest was beginning to feel tight and her head hurt but she wasn't about to complain to Cayden. If she got sick, there was a good chance she wouldn't recover. There was no medicine in the Border Lands, or anywhere for that matter.

Life was down to what could be done the old-fashioned way or nothing at all.

She had a feeling she was about to find out what it felt like to be at the mercy of a stranger.

Chapter Three

Cayden watched Nancy as she dozed after they'd eaten the squirrel stew Mike had warmed up for them. She hadn't eaten nearly as much as she should have and was sneezing and coughing now. The look on Mike's face mirrored his own worry. It was clear that she was sick and that was dangerous in the new world they lived in. With no medicine to use on her, she would have to either fight it and survive or succumb and die. He didn't want to lose her.

"She's sick, man," Mike said.

"I know." He wanted to hit the man for pointing out the obvious. "What can we do other than keep her warm?"

"She needs to drink plenty of liquids. I'll keep some weak broth warmed up, and we'll take turns forcing it and water down her. She's going to need to be turned frequently, or she'll end up with pneumonia if she doesn't already have it." Mike rattled off the instructions like he'd been through it before.

"It's just a bad cold, right?" Cayden asked.

"There's no just anything out here, man. You should know that. Everything is major when we don't have doctors or medicine or hospitals. You have to take everything seriously or you'll end up dying." Mike snapped out.

"I know that. I know that."

Cayden felt like a teenage boy instead of the twenty-six-year-old man he was. Seeing the love of his life sick and knowing he'd done this to her had just about reduced him to tears. Nancy meant everything to him. His Nan was his life. He'd do whatever it took to keep her safe from then on.

"Have you had trouble out here with black market hunters?" Cayden asked.

"Yes. It's been about a year since the last ones came through here, but that doesn't mean anything. I nearly lost my sister to them. We were just lucky that the neighbors showed up when they did, or I'd be dead and she'd be gone," Mike told him.

"Are those the neighbors you were talking about where your sister lives now?"

"Yeah. She's with them now. I'm thankful they were good men, and now I know she'll be safe with them. Plus, I'm just an hour away on foot. I'm getting one of their horses come spring. They've got three now that the yearling's gotten old enough to be ridden. That will cut down on the time it takes to get to their place."

"Was it hard to let her go?" Cayden asked.

"At first it was, but then it was a huge relief to know she'd be safe. She was so mad at me when she found out I'd signed over papers to them that I thought she'd never speak to me again after I finally got over the gunshot. It took a good three months but we're good now. She's happy and the guys are wonderful to her." Mike shrugged. "It had to be done."

"Yeah. I can see that."

Cayden thought about what Mike had said. He knew that he alone couldn't keep his Nan safe anymore. He'd nearly lost her once already and now she was sick because he hadn't been thinking straight. All he'd been able to think about at the time was getting her far away from anyone who'd take her from him. It had never occurred to him that he was walking her into something just as bad.

And they still had problems with black market raiders out here. What was he going to do? He realized in that moment that he needed another man to help him protect Nancy. The problem was finding someone he trusted and that would take time.

Cayden looked up when Mike returned with a small boiler he set next to the fire. He wondered if Mike could be that man. So far he'd been nothing but good to them. He'd saved their lives when he could have left them there to die. He hadn't known them or anything about them. They could have been thieves or anything, but he'd taken a chance and taken them in. Now he had a sick woman on his hands.

First he had to concentrate on getting his Nan well. Then he'd worry about the future. He couldn't make such an important decision without thinking long and hard on it. Plus, Nan had to feel comfortable with Mike before he'd even consider it.

He had a feeling that convincing her to allow another man into their relationship wasn't going to be easy. She'd been devastated and frightened beyond anything he'd seen when the "elders" of the commune they'd been living in had made their announcements about rotating the females between eight and ten men. He'd never seen her so distraught before.

I never want to see her that way again. But I can't take her safety for granted either.

There was nothing he could do about it right then. For now, Cayden had to focus on getting her well.

He shook her awake and offered her some water. She shook her head no, but he held it to her lips and demanded that she drink.

"You've got to drink it, Nan. You're going to get dehydrated if you don't. Don't make me force you, hon."

"Cold. Why am I so cold?" she asked after she'd taken a sip.

"You're sick, Nan. I let you get sick. You've got to help me get you well again. Drink some more," he told her.

He was pleased when she did, but knew it wasn't nearly enough. He'd have to wake her up again in a few minutes and make her drink more. Maybe the broth would be warm enough by then. He looked around, but didn't see Mike. The other man was probably taking care of chores. He should ask what he could do to help when Mike took over caring for his Nan. It was the least he could do.

The other man strode back in a few minutes later. "Has she had anything to drink?"

"She drank a few sips about fifteen minutes ago. I was going to wake her up in another ten or fifteen minutes and give her more," Cayden said.

"Get as much down her as you can. The broth should be ready by then. Test it to be sure it's not too hot. Hard to judge in that cast iron pot without trying it," Mike told him.

"Is there anything I can do to help you when you take over looking after her? I can bring in more firewood or if you've got a cow, I can milk it for you," he offered.

"I've tended the cow for the night. I might let you milk her in the morning. You'll have to shovel the path out there again, but I have a rope stretched from the back porch to the barn you can follow. There are chickens out there, as well. You can check for eggs while you're at it." Mike sat back on his heels and warmed his hands over the fire.

"How long have you lived here?"

"'Bout three years now. Place was a mess when my sister and I found it, but I've slowly gotten it in livable shape. Going to start putting some solar panels in come spring. They have them over at my sister's place. Be nice to have hot running water for showers," Mike said.

"Never thought about solar. I'm surprised they hadn't rigged them up at the commune we came from. Where do you get the supplies for them?" Cayden asked.

"There's a warehouse about four hours from here that they've been scavenging from. They said there's plenty for my place there unless someone's gotten to them by the time we can get back over there."

"How are you going to get them back?"

"They're going to hitch the horses to a wagon they repaired and one of them will go with me while the other stays home with Kate and their son, Jay."

Cayden smiled. "She has a child. That's great. I bet you're just as proud of him as she is."

Mike smiled. “Yeah. He reminds me of her when she was a baby. She’s pregnant again, too. I’m hoping it will be a little girl this time.”

“That’s great.”

Cayden gazed into the fire. The thought of Nancy having his baby sparked a fire inside of him he hadn’t felt before. The thought of raising a child hadn’t really crossed his mind. They’d been so intent on working at the commune then getting away, he hadn’t had time to consider the possibility.

A child meant more pressure to protect. The more he thought about it the more he knew for sure that Nancy needed another man in their lives to keep her and their children safe. The world out there was just too dangerous to try and do it alone.

He looked at Mike as he stirred the broth. Could he share his woman with him? Cayden didn’t know, but he had to make up his mind, and soon.

* * * *

“Enough. I can’t drink any more of it.” Nancy shook her head at him.

Mike sighed and set the broth down. She was drinking more each day, but he worried it wasn’t enough. Her cough had improved, as well, but a relapse would be deadly at this point.

“You can try again later. How are you feeling this morning?” he asked

“Better. My chest doesn’t hurt as much as it did. How long have I been sick?” she asked.

“Nearly a week now. You’ve about scared Cayden to death. He’s been by your side almost constantly. He’s sleeping right now.”

“I know your name is Mike and you saved us, but where are we?” she asked.

“In old Montana near Yellowstone. You’re lucky to be alive. Both of you. That dog saved your lives.”

"Where is he?" She turned her head to try and find the animal.

"He's upstairs sleeping with Cayden. I figure he thinks you're warm enough but he's sleeping right next to your man like he's making sure he stays warm. Never seen a dog act so protective before. Not even before everything went to hell."

She had a bout of coughing then settled again. He was pleased that she was able to talk more but knew she needed more rest. Mike rocked back on his heels. The woman was beautiful, with her shoulder length black hair that curled all around her face ant those amazing dark eyes that were like liquid pools of ink. She had a pert nose that was made for kissing and plump lips just as kissable.

It bothered him that he was so attracted to her. She was Cayden's woman, not his. The foolish man needed another man to help take care of her with how dangerous everything was nowadays, but that wasn't his business.

Can't help but wish it was, though. I could grow to care about her real easy.

But that wasn't going to happen. They'd be on their way once the snow melted. He doubted Cayden would want to stick around him with his woman. He liked the younger man, but didn't think he had an inkling of how to transform an old homestead into a livable home complete with a garden. It bothered him that they could end up going hungry in the end.

He briefly contemplated suggesting that they stay with him. He could use the help around the place and it would be easy to increase the size of the garden to accommodate more mouths to feed. But could he live alongside them and not end up with feelings for Nancy? He wasn't sure.

He picked up the broth and roused Nancy again. "Drink up. You need to regain your strength."

"I just drank some," she complained.

"I know, but you need to drink more. The more you drink each time, the longer I'll leave you alone to rest."

"You're being a bastard," she said, her brows knitting.

He chuckled. "I've been called worse. Drink up, Nancy. Calling me names isn't going to work on me."

She sighed and rolled her eyes. "Okay. I didn't mean it anyway. You've been good to us. Thank you."

She sipped the liquid until she'd managed to drink half the cup. Then she pulled back and shook her head.

"That's really all I can drink right now. I feel like my stomach is going to bust with that. I guess not eating for so long has shrunk my tummy," she said.

"Happens. We'll try you on some stew tomorrow if you're still doing this good. You need to start on solid food and regain your strength," Mike told her.

"Right now that doesn't even appeal to me, but maybe by tomorrow I'll think differently."

Mike sure hoped so. He covered Nancy back up to her neck and poked at the fire before adding another log. He needed to keep the fire going strong since he planned to take a short nap on the couch next to Nancy. She was doing well enough that he felt safe doing that. No doubt Cayden would be downstairs soon enough. The man was completely loyal and attentive to his woman. It was as it should be.

The first few days it had been impossible to get him to sleep anywhere except next to her, even when it was Mike's turn to watch over her. That told him just how much the other man loved his woman. Mike could easily see why, too. Not only was she beautiful, she was sweet and funny. In the short while he'd known her, he'd found that he liked her immensely. That was dangerous and would only lead to heartache. They'd be leaving come spring. How he'd keep from falling for her during the long winter months, Mike wasn't sure. He was heading for disappointment.

Chapter Four

"That was good, but I can't eat another bite." Nancy meant every word. The stew had been delicious, but she was full.

"You ate a good bit, hon. I'm proud of you." Cayden kissed the top of her head.

Nancy smiled at him. She adored him. He'd been so attentive, but then so had Mike. He didn't even know them and he'd taken them in and treated them like long lost friends. They owed their lives to the man, but maybe even beyond that, they owed their friendship to him.

"It's good to see your appetite coming back. You've lost a lot of weight since you've been sick," Mike told her.

Nancy was surprised he'd noticed. She had lost a good bit of weight. Her clothes hung on her. She'd been a little on the plump side before they'd left the commune so many months before. Now she was almost gaunt from nearly starving to death while she'd been so sick. She didn't mind losing the weight, but at this point, she felt puny and unattractive.

"I'll gain it back soon enough. Cayden will tell you that I like to cook and eat." She smiled over at Cayden.

"Your cooking is good, but you haven't had a roast until you've tasted hers," Cayden told the other man. "When she's feeling better you should let her cook you one."

"I'll take you up on that. I get tired of my own cooking. I eat at my sister's place every few weeks, but during the winter, I can't get over there at all," Mike told them.

"I'd be happy to cook while we're here once I've gotten back to my normal self," Nancy said a little shyly. She suddenly felt nervous for some reason.

"That would be great. When you're feeling better, that is," Mike said.

"I'm going to go see about the cow and chickens for the night," Cayden said.

"I can do that," Mike said, standing.

"My turn. I don't mind. You can keep Nancy company while I'm gone."

Nancy watched Cayden walk out of the living room toward what she'd learned was the kitchen. She missed him when he was gone, but had begun to feel comfortable around Mike the last few days. The man was handsome in an entirely different way than her Cayden. He wasn't quite as tall but very muscular with wide shoulders and a trim waist. His sandy, light brown hair complemented the hazel of his eyes.

She felt drawn to the man despite her reminder that she loved Cayden. It made her a little nervous around the man though he'd given her no reason to be. He'd been the perfect gentleman so far.

The dog whined and laid his head on her lap where she was propped up against the couch. Though the dog didn't belong to them, he'd adopted them from day one, it seemed. Anytime Cayden was out tending to the cow or bringing in wood, the dog would lie next to her or rest his head in her lap. She laughed and rubbed him.

"You're spoiled rotten, and I don't even know you."

"Other than to go out to do his business, he hasn't left your side since I brought you in here," Mike told her.

"He's sweet. Big, but sweet."

"I think he's a Newfoundland or an Irish Wolfhound mix of some sort. You're right though, he's huge."

"He's cute."

Mike chuckled. "I don't know about cute, but he is loyal. Until he got to know me, he didn't let me near you without Cayden being close by. Now he's a little more trusting of me. It's hard to believe he wasn't yours to begin with."

"Cayden said he figured we stumbled into his home when we squeezed between those rocks to seek shelter," Nancy said.

"That's probably true. One thing is for certain. He's adopted you as his family."

"He'll be good for protection. I won't feel nearly as scared when Cayden goes off hunting with him close by."

"It's not safe for you to be by yourself at all," Mike said.

"I know, but there isn't much choice with the two of us. I tried going with him, and he never saw anything with me tagging along. I guess between the two of us our scents scared off any game."

"Just isn't safe," Mike mumbled then stood again. "I'm going to wash up these dishes. I'll just be in the other room if you need me."

Nancy watched him go. He was a solitary man. He didn't talk a whole lot, but had begun to open up a little more each day she'd been able to sit up and talk. She liked him. That thought surprised her since she'd begun to distrust men in general, with the exception of Cayden. Men she'd thought she'd known and trusted back at the commune had turned into strangers with a word from the leaders. It was enough to sour anyone against them.

Cayden was sweet and careful with her. He never lost his temper and encouraged her when she wasn't sure about what she was doing. She loved that about him. But then she loved just about everything about him.

Mike was more stoic and careful about what he said and did. Everything appeared deliberate, as if he'd thought long and hard before doing it. He struck her as a solid, steadfast sort of man who you could depend on to always do the right thing. He'd certainly proved that with them.

And if Nancy was honest with herself, that appealed to her. So did his handsome good looks. That worried her. She didn't feel right noticing how his light brown hair had sandy highlights, especially in the firelight. She thought his hazel eyes twinkled at times when she'd said something particularly humorous. His broad shoulders and narrow hips appealed to her. That stopped her. Why would she think about how he looked when she had Cayden?

Nancy shook her head. She was thinking nonsense. Cayden was her man and he was just as dependable. He'd remained by her side despite everything that had been against them.

The dog whined and nudged her arm. She smiled and petted him. It looked like the big cuddly animal could tell when she was thinking too hard.

"We really need to name you. What do you want to be called? Something strong and fitting for a hero like yourself." She ruffled his hair and tried out several names. "Hercules, Big Ben, Max, Butch, Bruno, Duke. None of those really fit."

She thought about how he'd saved them and how attentive he was. Something had to fit. Then she thought about some of her favorite books and settled on Galahad. He was a noble beast and the name fit for her.

"You must be talking to the dog," Mike said as he strode into the room.

"I was trying to figure out what to call him. I decided on Galahad," she said with a smile.

"Guess that fits. He saved you and Cayden. Knight-like qualities if I ever saw any."

"I think he likes his name." Nancy laughed when the dog licked her cheek.

"Cayden should be back inside soon. Think you can sit up on the couch for a while so I can change out the bedding?" Mike asked.

"Yeah. I feel good. All that good food has helped." She felt heat burn her cheeks at the blatant compliment she'd given him.

"Yeah, well. It's nourishing and you needed that." Mike brushed it off and helped her to stand.

Nancy could admit she was unsteady on her feet. It had been a while since she'd stood. She was sure without Mike's help she would have fallen. He wrapped one arm around her waist as he helped her take the few steps it took to sit down. He turned her and lowered her to the cushions. Once again, heat burned her face at the almost intimate touch of his hands on her.

"How's that?" he asked.

"Good."

Mike covered her up with a blanket then settled a pillow behind her to help prop her up. Then he gathered the dirty bedding and carried it out of the room. A few minutes later he returned and took the stairs to the second floor. When he came back, he had an armful of fresh linen and blankets.

It took him no time to make up another pallet on the floor. She hated that he had to do all of that, but she honestly didn't have the strength to help him.

I wish I wasn't so weak. I want to do something to support myself like Cayden is.

Well, she'd make it up to him when she was able to cook and wash for him. She'd make sure he had good meals and clean clothes. Nancy realized that idea really excited her. Why? Was it just because she wanted to repay him for his kindness, or was she beginning to like him more than she should?

Most women out here have two or three men to keep them safe. Maybe it's okay that I feel a sort of attachment to him. It doesn't mean anything. I'm Cayden's woman. That isn't going to change.

Still, the thought worried her. Cayden seemed to pick up on her frame of mind when he returned from tending the cow and chickens.

"Is something wrong, Nancy?" he asked, settling next to her on the couch.

"No. Just frustrated that I'm so weak still. I want to be able to help instead of sitting here like a useless piece of junk."

"That's not true. You're still recovering from nearly dying, hon. Give it time and you'll be back to doing your usual things. I can't wait for you to cook for Mike. He's going to never want us to leave once he gets a taste of your cooking."

"Do you think we could find a place near here? I mean we already know Mike, and his sister is close by. It would be nice to be able to have another woman to talk to occasionally," she said.

"I agree. We'll talk to Mike about it closer to springtime. He may know of a place or maybe his sister's men will know of a house close by."

* * * *

Cayden watched the way Mike acted around Nancy. The man was careful not to startle her and paid close attention when she spoke. He thought there was an attraction there that the other man was fighting hard to ignore. It was in the way he watched her and catered to her that gave him away. The idea of the other man being attracted to her didn't bother Cayden like he knew it should.

If there was the least bit of attraction between the two of them, he knew he would eventually approach the man about joining with him to keep Nancy safe. He'd been thinking a lot about the idea over the last few days. He'd nearly gotten her killed and had done a poor job of keeping her fed, as well. It really did take two men to keep a woman safe in the environment they were living in now.

What will it feel like to watch Mike kiss her? Will it make me angry? Will I be jealous when she kisses him back?

Cayden didn't know how he'd feel to see them together. Right now, it only worried him. He wasn't sure how he'd feel when it became a reality. If it became a reality. The other man might not be interested at all. But Cayden doubted that. Mike paid closer attention to his Nancy than a man who had no interest in a woman did. It would be all about timing.

For now, he would encourage the other man to spend time with Nancy without appearing too obvious about it. He shook his head. How he was going to do that, Cayden had no idea. All he knew was that he wanted the two of them to get to know each other well before spring came.

"How are you feeling?" he asked Nancy as he sat down on the couch next to her.

"Good. I'm getting stronger every day now. When are you going to let me off this couch to cook? I feel like a slacker just sitting here all day every day. I need to get up to get my strength back."

"I think you can walk around the room some during the day now. I'll talk to Mike to see what he thinks. He seems to know more about taking care of you than I do."

"That's not true, Cayden. You've done the best you could considering what we've been dealing with." She smiled up at him. "Getting caught in a blizzard wasn't your fault. We needed to keep moving so those men couldn't catch up with us."

"Still, we should have stayed at the half-way house where there was food and shelter. I made a mistake that nearly cost you your life, Nancy. I trust Mike to know what's best for you."

She appeared a little uneasy when he said that. Why? Cayden hoped the other man didn't scare her. So far she hadn't appeared to be afraid of him. Had he said something that bothered her?

Galahad chose that moment to lay his head on their touching thighs and look up at them. Cayden laughed. The big guy seemed to always know when one of them was worrying about something.

"What is it, boy? Do you need to go out? It's cold as crap." Cayden rubbed the dog's head.

Galahad just huffed out a breath and lay down in front of them. Obviously he didn't want out. He just wanted to reassure them he was there if they needed him. The dog was truly remarkable. He didn't look to be much over a couple of years old so someone somewhere was missing him. He had to have been raised by someone. No wild dog would be so caring around humans.

"I think he's just craving attention," Nancy said, her smile a ray of sunshine.

"I think you're probably right."

Mike walked into the room and checked the fire. Cayden looked from Nancy to the other man and noticed how her eyes were drawn to him. It was a good sign to Cayden. He didn't dwell on why he was willing to contemplate sharing the woman he loved with the other man. He just knew it was the right thing to do. Mike had been nothing but good to them. He had no doubt he'd be good to Nancy should things work out.

"Nancy is chomping at the bit to get into the kitchen. Do you think she's strong enough now?" Cayden asked.

Mike turned and looked at them with a thoughtful expression. "Yeah. I think so, but only with one of us with her for now. I don't want her legs to give out and she fall."

"I agree. She's been either on the pallet or on the couch for nearly two weeks now. I'm sure her stamina is low."

"Can I get up now? Both of you are here. Please." Nancy clapped her hands together.

"Yeah. Cayden, you walk with her." Mike nodded at him.

Cayden stood then helped Nancy up next to him. She wobbled a bit then seemed to find her legs and started walking around the couch. The smile on her face was well worth it. They circled the couch twice then she headed for the bathroom.

"Where are you going?" Cayden asked.

"I'm going to the bathroom while I'm up. There's no need for one of you to carry me since I'm up anyway," she said.

Mike scowled at her but nodded. It was obvious that he hated for her to be out of his sight so soon after getting up.

Cayden waited outside the bathroom while she was inside. When it seemed to take longer than was necessary, he knocked on the door and called out to her.

"Nancy? Are you okay in there?"

"I'm fine. Give me a few minutes. I'm washing my face. I haven't been able to do that myself in weeks."

"You're pushing it, woman. I don't want you to overdo it," he said.

"I'm fine. I'll be out in a minute."

Cayden frowned. She'd deliberately maneuvered him into this. He'd forgotten that she had a way of getting her way when she wanted to. Sometimes it was cute, but times like this, he worried that she'd end up in trouble. He looked over to where Mike stood next to the fire with an odd smile on his face.

"What are you grinning about?" he demanded.

"She's smart. Got what she wanted, didn't she?" Mike asked.

"Yeah," Cayden acknowledged.

The door to the bathroom opened and Nancy shuffled out. Her face held a glow, showing that she'd scrubbed it good and though there was a smile on her face, her eyes showed that she was tired.

"Let's get you back to the couch before you collapse," Cayden said.

"I'm ready. Thanks for letting me clean up a bit. I really needed that." Nancy allowed Cayden to wrap an arm around her waist and help her back to the couch.

When she'd sunk down with a sigh, Cayden relaxed. She'd definitely pushed it this first time. He'd have to be more diligent when she got up the next time. He should have known she'd wanted more than just to use the bathroom.

"I'm going to start dinner. Afraid it's going to be venison again tonight. I do have some potatoes and carrots to put with it though."

"I'm not choosey a bit, Mike. Anything you fix is good to me," Nancy told him.

"Same here," Cayden added.

"Wish I had another rabbit, but they're not coming out much in the snow. Hard to trap one in it, too," Mike said over his shoulder as he walked toward the kitchen.

Cayden sat down next to Nancy. "He's really been good to us, hasn't he?"

"Yes. I'm still a little surprised, considering he didn't know us. He's a compassionate man. It's too bad he doesn't have a woman of his own. He'd take good care of her," Nancy said.

"I think he would, too. I like him." Cayden wanted to explore how Nancy felt about the other man, but didn't want to push her too much.

"I sure hope we can find a place close by. He'd be a good person to know, and it sounds like his sister and her men would be great, as well. Being close to others would give us a little more security," Nancy told him.

"I'd feel better if there was another man with us, Nancy. I worry, leaving you alone when I have to go out to hunt," he said without looking at her.

"Another man? You mean like living with us?" Her voice held a bit of a squeak to it.

"Yeah. It seems like out here everyone lives in threes or fours for safety. I can see where that would be safer," he said.

"Like living with us?" she repeated.

"Yeah. Like a family."

"Cayden. I don't know."

"I know, hon. Just think about it. I worry about you."

"I have Galahad now."

"He's just a dog. He might be able to attack another man intent on hurting or taking you, but if there were two of them, or they had weapons, he wouldn't stand a chance." Cayden looked over at her this time and reached out to squeeze her hand. "Just think about it."

Chapter Five

"Damn cow."

Mike wiped the milk off his hands and stood. The Jersey hadn't wanted to stand still for him that morning. Made for a messy milking. Just what he'd needed today. The start of an early thaw had made the still snow-covered ground slippery. Now he had a bucket of milk and a basket of eggs to keep from spilling as he navigated the slick path.

He had no doubt it wouldn't last long. It was only the end of January or thereabouts. They had another month of snow to contend with. It wouldn't start thawing for real until mid-March. This was just a worrisome speck of time they'd have to deal with until the temperatures zeroed out once again. In the meantime, he'd have to make sure the two guests of his understood that it wouldn't last long. They had a lot to learn about the Montana winters.

Guests. They didn't really feel like guests any longer. They felt like part of his life now. Somehow over the last few weeks, they'd wormed their way into his heart without doing one damn thing to accomplish it. He liked both of them, and if he were completely honest with himself, he cared more than was right for Nancy. She belonged to Cayden, but Mike had feelings for her now, as well.

I'm crazy for letting her get to me. They'll leave come spring, and I'll be by myself again. I sure as hell don't need to be pining after someone else's woman.

But he feared it was too late. He loved her thick black hair that curled around her face and down to her shoulders. Her golden skin was dark compared to his much lighter complexion. She was curvy and soft all over. Just the way he enjoyed a woman. But she wasn't his to claim.

Mike carefully made his way back to the house, slipping several times but managing not to lose the precious milk and eggs as he righted himself and continued on. Today Nancy was going to cook for them. He'd wanted her to rest a few days longer, but she'd pleaded so sweetly to be able to cook that he'd agreed once Cayden had.

She did things to him. Things that made him want to give her whatever she wanted that was in his power.

That was dangerous. In a lot of ways.

He stomped his feet at the back door to clear them of the muddy snow clinging to them so he didn't track it into the kitchen. Once inside, he set the milk and eggs down before toeing off his boots and hanging up his coat and scarf.

"It looks nasty out there," Cayden said, walking into the kitchen seconds later. "Will it get cold again?"

"Yeah. This is just a small thaw. We've got another month or so of hard winter left ahead of us. Don't be fooled by this. It will be below zero again before you know it."

"I figured as much. I've always heard that it can snow any time of the year out here," Cayden said.

"What's Nancy doing?" Mike asked.

"She's upstairs looking through the clothes you told her about to see if anything will fit. Her clothes are beginning to get a bit threadbare."

"Whoever lived here had at least two daughters, if not more. There were tons of women's clothes in several of the closets. Most of them seemed large enough for Nancy." Mike set the milk on the counter next to the eggs.

Whatever Nancy didn't use to cook with, he'd set in the cold box outside on the porch for later. He kept meat and the excess milk and eggs out there where they would stay cold but where wild animals wouldn't be able to get to them.

"Hey, Cayden. I'm ready to come down now. I found quite a few things I can wear." Nancy called out in an excited voice.

"I'll go with you to help bring them down. I don't want Nancy carrying anything. She might get overbalanced and fall," Mike said.

"Good idea," the other man said.

Mike followed Cayden into the living room and upstairs where Nancy waited with an air of excitement about her. He liked seeing her smile and enjoyed knowing that he had even a little part in putting it on her face.

"Looks like you found a lot of things you can wear. I'll wash them up for you and we'll hang them by the fire to dry," Mike said.

"Thanks for letting me go through them. Are you sure your sister doesn't need them?" she asked for the third time.

"She's got plenty of clothes. Most of the ones up there wouldn't have fit her anyway. You've obviously lost a lot of weight after being ill. I thought they might fit at least until you gain some weight back." Mike picked up a small pile and started down the stairs ahead of them.

"I hope I don't gain much back. I was kind of pudgy before. I like being smaller," Nancy said.

"You need some meat on your bones, woman," Cayden teased.

Mike agreed, but it wasn't his place to say anything. Nancy wasn't his. Deep down he wished she was though. Hopefully they'd settle down somewhere close so he could help keep her safe. The idea of something happening to her didn't sit well with him. Cayden needed help caring for her, but suggesting that to the other man probably wouldn't go over well with him.

Once they'd returned to the living room, Mike gathered all of the clothes up and carried them to the laundry area where he'd set up two large plastic tubs. He'd heat up water to wash them in then rinse and hang them up to dry. He noted that among the two pairs of jeans and four shirts there were women's undergarments. Thoughts of seeing

Nancy in the lacy panties and bra had his dick hard and his balls aching.

Mike cursed under his breath then nearly jumped out of his skin when Nancy walked in.

"Hey, why don't you let me wash them? I feel fine and I'm tired of watching you and Cayden do everything."

"You're going to cook for us tonight. That's enough to start. I don't mind washing these. It won't take long," he said, quickly burying the undergarments in the pile.

If she'd noticed that he'd been eyeing them when she walked in, she didn't show it. Instead she shoved him aside with her hips and pulled out the jeans first.

"Go warm up some water for me. I've got this." She smiled up at him and the earth moved under his feet.

Mike couldn't say anything, his voice completely failing him. Instead, he merely nodded and escaped from the tiny room to do as she'd said. The feel of her body touching his had generated sparks that had his blood coursing through his body like cars around a racetrack. Why did she affect him like that when she wasn't his? Letting them leave come spring was going to hurt like hell. He still had another month or two of spending time with her, with them before that happened.

Holy fuck, he was screwed.

Once he'd warmed up the water, Mike returned to pour it into the large tub for her. He dipped up more clean snow and set it on the hearth to heat up, as well. She'd need it to rinse the clothes.

"Mike? Is the other water ready?" Nancy called out.

"Just about. I'll bring it through in a few minutes."

Instead, he was going to get Cayden to do it. He didn't need any more time alone with her than he'd already had. His libido was driving him crazy to touch her, kiss her, make her his. She wasn't his. She was Cayden's and he needed to remember that.

Cayden walked in seconds later and laughed. "She talked you into letting her wash the clothes, didn't she?"

"Yeah." Mike couldn't help the sheepish expression he knew colored his face. "Here, take the water to her."

"I ought to make you do it since you caved to her. Glad I'm not the only one who can't say no to her." Cayden grabbed the hot pads and picked up the large pot of hot water and walked into the laundry area.

Mike sighed and added another log to the fire. He'd need to bring in more wood before the day was over. Already his stomach growled at the thought of Nancy cooking for them. She'd need more wood to do that. He sighed. Might as well do it now rather than later.

* * * *

"Please. I'm sick of being stuck inside. You and Mike go out every day to see about the cow and chickens and to get wood. I haven't been out since we got here." Nancy was dying to go outside for just a few minutes.

"Mike, what do you think? If we bundle her up she should be okay for just a few minutes, right?" Cayden asked.

"I guess. I don't like it. She just got over nearly dying," the other man said.

"I'm well now. Just for a little while. I want to smell the fresh air and feel the snow crunch under my feet. Please, guys." She wasn't above begging.

"Fine. Let's get you bundled up," Cayden told her.

Nancy looked over at Mike. She really wanted him to agree, as well. She wasn't sure why, but she did.

"Okay," Mike said. "She needs thermals under her clothes, then she can use my bigger coat over all of that."

She grinned up at the man then quickly turned her smile to Cayden. What was wrong with her? She shouldn't feel so happy that

Mike had agreed to let her go outside. He wasn't who she wanted to please. Was he?

I'm really going stir crazy being inside all this time. I'm thinking about Mike as if I need his approval as well as Cayden's. That's insane. Cayden and I are a family. Not Mike and Cayden and I.

She hurried to follow Cayden into the living room where he helped her undress then pull on thermals, followed by her jeans and the long sleeved flannel shirt she'd found that probably had been a man's at some point. She felt way overdressed even before Mike held out his massive coat to her. She let him help her into it then sat on a chair while Cayden helped her put on the boots she'd found that were only a size too large for her. With the two pairs of socks on her feet they pretty much fit now.

"Do I pass muster?" she asked both men.

Cayden gave her a thumbs up while Mike only shrugged. She took it as an affirmative and grinned.

"Remember. We're only staying out for a few minutes so you can get some fresh air and settle those jumping beans in your feet for a while," Mike muttered as he led the way out the back door and off the porch.

Galahad followed, bounding out into the snow like a crazed monster of a rabbit. Nancy giggled.

"Wow. Look how pretty the snow is." Nancy turned around to take in the sheer beauty of the landscape. Everything was covered in the pure white stuff. "Listen. It's so quiet out here."

"The snow acts as a buffer so that you only hear loud noises and not the softer ones," Mike told her.

"Walk around some, hon. You can't be out much longer," Cayden told her.

"Let's build a snowman," Nancy said.

"No. We aren't going to be out that long," Mike said. "Do what Cayden said and walk around a little bit."

Nancy stuck her tongue out at both men and bent down to grab some snow. She rolled it into a ball and threw it at Cayden. He yelped then shook his head.

"You're not going to lure me into a snowball fight with you. You don't need to get cold and wet." Cayden brushed off the snow.

She rolled another snowball in her hands, but this time she lobbed it at Mike. He turned so that it splattered against his back. She kept on throwing them until Mike chased her down and wrapped his arms around her to stop her from doing it. Galahad barked and ran around the three of them with as much enthusiasm as Nancy felt.

"That's enough, brat. It's time to go inside. You can't behave, so inside you go." Mike looked down at her with his arms tightly wound around her.

Nancy couldn't help but feel a thrill race down her spine at the closeness of the man. She hadn't expected to feel anything for him other than annoyance that he'd put a stop to her fun, but she did. From the expression on his face, he felt it, as well. For a second, Nancy thought he might kiss her, but then he was releasing her and stepping back.

"Inside, young lady. You've played around enough."

She looked over to where Cayden stood watching them with something strange on his face. Was he angry with them? She prayed she hadn't done something that would mess everything up. She'd only meant to have a little fun. Now she worried she'd hurt Cayden somehow. She was sure he'd seen how she'd looked at Mike. Had her emotions shown on her face so that he knew she'd been looking for the man to kiss her? Nancy prayed he hadn't.

It took both men calling to get Galahad to go inside once she walked back into the house. It was obvious that she wasn't the only one not happy about the short romp out in the snow.

"Help her out of that jacket and be sure she's dry underneath it all. She can't afford to get sick again. I'll be upstairs." Mike's short tone said that he wasn't happy about what had happened outside.

"Thanks for letting me go out, guys. I needed that." Nancy hoped they both knew just how thankful she was.

Mike just grunted and continued into the other room. Cayden helped her off with the gloves, coat, and scarf, then urged her into the living room where he helped her undress in front of the fire.

"You don't need to wear the thermals inside where it's warm enough. We'll save those for when you go outside again." Cayden folded them before helping her dress in her jeans and the T-shirt she wore under the long sleeved blouse she'd had on earlier.

"I think Mike is mad at me for trying to start a snowball fight," Nancy said.

"He's just worried about you getting sick again. You nearly died, honey. I could have lost you. This cold isn't something you can take lightly," Cayden said.

"I know. I wasn't planning on rolling in the snow, just make a snowman or throw a few snowballs. He never smiles, Cayden. I wanted him to smile like you do. Maybe that's wrong of me." Nancy wasn't sure why she'd decided to tell Cayden that, but there it was.

"He's lived by himself for several years now, Nancy. I doubt he's had much to smile about. Did he act upset when he grabbed you earlier?" Cayden asked without looking at her.

"I—I don't know. He didn't at first, but then he made us come inside. Then he left and went upstairs in a hurry."

"He's just giving you time to dress in private. That's all. He'll be back down soon," Cayden said. "Now what's for dinner tonight? I worked up an appetite."

"You didn't do anything out there except try to avoid my snowballs," Nancy teased.

"That was hard work."

Nancy punched him in the arm then walked into the kitchen to decide what to cook. Considering they only had deer meat, the options were going to be limited. Maybe deer smothered in gravy with cornbread. Wasn't much, but it would be filling.

She couldn't help but think back over the few seconds when Mike had held her in his arms outside. At first he'd looked annoyed then he'd looked surprised as he'd slowly lowered his head but caught himself before he'd done something neither of them would be able to take back. Why was she so attracted to him? She loved Cayden and never wanted to hurt him. Was it just because they'd been around each other so much over the last month? Being constantly in each other's company had to be the reason. They spent a lot of time around each other.

Nancy tried to write it off as nothing but the close proximity, but deep down, she knew she was attracted to the other man and that scared her.

A hell of a lot.

Chapter Six

"I'll be fine, hon. Mind Mike while I'm gone," Cayden said as he bundled up.

"You don't have to go hunting, Cayden. I'm used to the area around here," Mike told him.

"You've been doing the majority of the work while we've been living with you. I can hunt. I'm good with a bow," Cayden said.

Nancy knew he would be fine, but she couldn't help but worry. There were wolves out there as well as bears. Then again, she'd been nervous when Mike had gone out hunting, as well. It was only natural she'd worry about either man while they were gone. It didn't mean anything.

"Take Galahad with you Cayden. That way I won't worry as much," Nancy said.

"If he'll leave you he can come along. That dog is usually glued to your side."

"That's a good idea, Nancy," Mike said.

"Hurry back," Nancy said, giving Cayden a tight hug.

"I'll be back before you know it." Cayden picked up the bow and slung the quiver over his shoulder.

Nancy watched him trudge through the snow through the window until he disappeared into the woods. She prayed he'd be successful and come back to her safely.

"He'll be fine, Nancy. I wish he'd let me go instead, but he wanted to do it," Mike said. "Come on back into the living room. It's cold in here."

Nancy let him take her arm and pull her into the other room. She knew it would be hours before Caleb would return, even if he killed something quickly. He'd have to field dress it before packing it back. That could easily take over an hour. She sighed and plopped down on the couch.

"Want some hot tea?" Mike asked.

"That would be wonderful. Thanks."

Minutes later, he handed her a mug of the dandelion tea and Nancy cupped it to warm her hands as she sipped. Mike held a similar mug and sat next to her on the couch. She couldn't help but be aware of him so close to her. His scent reminded her of wood smoke and fresh pine. He smelled of winter and man.

She thought about how Cayden smelled to her. His was lighter, less woodsy, more like the ocean and warm summer days. How could they each smell so different yet she was attracted to each of them.

I might as well admit it to myself. I'm attracted to Mike and can't seem to do a thing about it. Why? He's so different from Cayden.

Maybe it was because of that difference. Where Cayden was light-hearted and always upbeat, Mike was quiet and more down to earth, always looking at the possible outcomes before making a decision.

Cayden smiled more readily than Mike, and was always trying to make her smile. Mike's smiles were rare but when they came, they were genuine and breathtaking. He tended to worry about everything, and was always reminding them that things were different in the Border Lands.

Nancy appreciated Mike for saving them and taking them in, but she also appreciated his kindness though it was often masked in gruffness, and she was attracted to his quiet masculinity. Had she not caught glimpses of that beneath his staunch exterior, she might have been uncomfortable around him, maybe even a little frightened of him. He was all male and often reminded her of what she'd thought mountain men would be like.

Still, she liked him.

She was attracted to him and that didn't seem to be changing or going away. It bothered her. The thought of moving on once spring arrived bothered her. She didn't want to move away unless it was close to where Mike lived.

That knowledge made her feel guilty. She was Cayden's woman. She wasn't Mike's. Could never be his.

Could she?

"What are you thinking about so hard over there?" Mike's deep voice startled her.

"Oh. Nothing, really. Just about where we'll find a home once it gets to be spring. We'll need to find one close by so we'll have time to dig up a garden," she said.

"There are a few houses nearby, but they'll need a lot of work to make them ready for next winter," Mike told her.

"I'd like to be close to you and your sister. It would be nice to have another woman to talk to sometimes." Nancy didn't add that she didn't want to move too far from him, as well.

"I think you'd get along great with her."

"If she's anything like you, I'm sure I will."

"Like me? Well, we're not a lot alike. You'll probably feel more comfortable around her," he said.

"Why do you say that? You don't make me feel uncomfortable." Nancy cocked her head and watched him.

Mike shrugged. "I can be pretty hard-nosed at times, or so she tells me."

Nancy laughed. "Yeah, I can see that, but it's only when you're worried about something. Like when I wanted to go outside. You were pretty stubborn about that."

Mike shrugged. "I was worried you'd get sick again."

"I've been out several times since then, and I haven't gotten sick yet. You and Cayden make sure I stay warm and dry. Getting outside some has helped keep me from going stir crazy and the fresh air had to be good for me."

Mike rolled his eyes and shook his head. “Like you keep saying every time you want to go out. You’ve gotten your way, brat. Don’t harp on it, or I’ll say no next time.”

She grinned. “I bet you’d give in if I begged and batted my eyes at you.”

“Not a chance. I’m immune to womanly wiles.”

“Even when I pout?”

“Especially when you pout. Why do you think I walk off when you start that? I let Cayden deal with you when you do that.”

“Exactly. You can’t handle it so you run way.”

“I said walk away, not run,” he admonished.

“Semantics. Regardless, you know you can’t hold out with me so you *walk* away and leave poor Cayden to deal with me. I think you’re afraid you’ll give in, as well.” Nancy grinned at him.

“You’re a little brat. If you were mine, I’d turn you over my knee when you act like that,” Mike said, frowning at her.

“You’d spank me when I was bad?” she laughed, and batted her eyelashes at him.

“Don’t tempt me, Nancy,” he said in a growly voice.

Nancy realized that was exactly what she wanted to do.

Tempt him.

Chapter Seven

Mike felt as if he were holding on to his control by a thin piece of sodden spaghetti. He was sure at any second it would snap, and he'd lose control and show Nancy just how much he couldn't say no to her. She was playing with fire, teasing him when he was already super aware of her as a woman. Cayden's woman.

He stood to check the fire at the same time she stood up saying she needed to run to the bathroom. They slammed into each other. Mike steadied her, but didn't let her go even though she was pressed tightly against him. They remained like that for long moments. As he stared down into her startled eyes, he lowered his head and pressed his lips to hers.

It was her sudden intake of breath that jerked him away from her, as if that one brief touch of their lips had created an electrical spark. And maybe it had. He sure as hell felt like he'd been shocked.

"I'm sorry. That shouldn't have happened." He took a step back, then another one. "I'm going to bring in some more firewood."

Mike turned and all but ran out the back door, forgetting to grab his coat in the process. It wasn't until he'd reached the wood stack ten feet from the back door and knee deep in snow that he realized he wasn't wearing his coat or his boots.

"Mike!"

He looked up to a very worried Nancy. She held his coat on the back steps. She hadn't even noticed that he was sock footed.

Mike grabbed two logs and walked back to the back porch.

"You shouldn't be out here without a coat, Mike. You'll get sick." Nancy held out his coat then noticed his wet sock feet. "Oh, my God,

Mike. Come in this instant. You need dry socks on. Why did you run out there without your boots on?"

"Trying to get away from you," he muttered.

She jerked back. "I—I'm sorry."

Mike cursed when she dropped the coat over his arm and turned to shuffle back into the house.

Damn it all, he'd hurt her feelings. Fuck, he was such a screw-up. Now she thought it was all her fault. He'd been the one to kiss her. It hadn't been the other way around. Yeah, she'd flirted with him, but he should have seen it for what it was. She'd just been trying to be friendly when he was always so damn hard-nosed around her.

Because I know that if I let down my guard something like that kiss would have happened a lot sooner.

Now he'd gone and made things worse. Knowing that he'd hurt her dug at his chest like a garden spade. He loved seeing her smile, and had enjoyed her teasing, but too much of it made him lose control, and he couldn't do that. Cayden would serve him his balls on a platter if he knew Mike had kissed his woman, and rightfully so.

Mike would have to make sure he was never alone with Nancy again. He'd do all the outside work from now on. Cayden would just have to deal with it.

By the time he'd replaced his wet socks and restocked the wood pile on the back porch, several hours had gone by. He returned inside to find Nancy sitting in front of the fire brushing her hair. She'd evidently taken a quick bath.

"Did you carry the water upstairs by yourself?" he asked in surprise.

"No, I used the sink to wash my hair. It was driving me crazy. I doubt I could have carried water all the way upstairs. Just carting it from in here to the kitchen was hard enough." She gave him a weak smile.

"Next time, tell me and I'll fix you a hot bath so you can soak for a while." He watched as she slowly drew the brush through her hair and his dick hardened.

Fuck. Did everything about her have to make him hard? How was he going to make it another month with her under the same roof without screwing everything up? Nancy didn't need to worry about him attacking her. He wanted her to feel safe in his house. What was he going to say to Cayden if she told him about the kiss?

The truth. I tell him that I'm attracted to her, but that I was going to be damn sure that never happened again.

He wondered if she would tell Cayden or pretend it had never happened. He sure as hell couldn't pretend. He could still taste her on his lips. She tasted warm and sweet and her scent nearly had his eyes crossing at how good she'd smelled. There was the hint of something citrusy when he'd inhaled while they'd been close.

He groaned and turned away from the sight of her bathed in the firelight. He needed to keep his distance while Cayden was hunting.

"I'm going to check on the cow. She might need more hay."

"Remember your boots and coat this time," she said without looking up.

He felt the corner of his mouth lift at her subtle teasing. Even after the kiss she was still light and teasing. Mike refused to think about what that might mean. It didn't matter. He needed to remember she was Cayden's woman. Not his.

* * * *

The minute Cayden stepped into the house, he could sense the unease in Mike. The other man was standing by the stove pouring a cup of tea. He frowned and glanced toward the living room. Was Nancy okay? Had something happened to her?

"Nancy," he called out. "I'm back."

Galahad walked in behind him, shaking snow from his fur all over the kitchen floor. Cayden winced.

Nancy raced from the living room and hurled herself into his arms. It rocked him back a step as he closed his arms around her.

"Did you kill anything?" she asked.

"Yep. Got a four point that should give us enough food for at least eight or nine days."

"I'm so glad you're back safe. I was worried about you," she told him.

"I'll help you with the deer," Mike said, setting his tea down. "We need to get it cut up and put away before something gets wind of it."

"I could use something warm to drink before we go back out. Is that tea?" he asked.

"Yeah." Mike pulled down another mug and poured some for him.

Cayden sensed that something was up with him. Had he and Nancy fought about something? He knew Nancy could be stubborn when she wanted something. Had she wanted to go back outside while he'd been gone? Whatever it was, it had Mike on edge. Nancy seemed a little uneasy, as well.

Five minutes later, he and Mike started work on the deer that they'd hung on the hook roped to the tree limb for just such a purpose.

"Is something wrong, Mike?" Cayden finally asked.

"Yeah. I need to tell you something, but I'd prefer you set your knife down first."

Cayden frowned. "What the hell?" But he dropped the knife into the bucket they were using for the meat they cut off the deer.

"I doubt Nancy is going to say anything, but you have a right to know," Mike began.

"Know what?"

Silence.

Cayden watched Mike seem to struggle with something. Then he seemed to settle.

"I kissed Nancy." He sighed and continued speaking. "It won't happen again. I don't know what happened, but she's not to blame. It was all me."

Cayden had to bite back a grin. This was more than he could have hoped. Nature was doing all the prep work for him.

"Say something. Do you want to hit me? 'Cause I sure would want to kick your ass if she were my woman."

"It's okay, Mike."

"The fuck it is. She's your woman. You should be pissed as hell."

"I've been wanting to talk to you about something for a few days now, but didn't know how to broach the subject."

Mike thrust his hands on his hips and glared at him. The other man honestly wanted him to be angry about the situation. Maybe he should be, but after everything that had happened, he couldn't. He wanted Nancy safe. He loved her that much.

"What has that got to do with the fact that I kissed your woman?" Mike demanded.

"It's obvious that I can't keep her safe on my own. I nearly lost her because I don't know what the hell I'm doing and if another group of poachers show up while we're on our own in the spring, they'll probably succeed in killing me and taking her. I need help keeping her safe."

"What has that got to do with anything?"

"Most of the families around here are made up of two or more men caring for a single woman. That's what I need for Nancy. I want you to be the other man," Cayden finally got out.

"What?"

"You heard me. I want to share Nancy with you, Mike. I trust you, and you've proved that you know how to take care of her. The fact that you kissed her shows that you're attracted to her."

"You should be pissed as hell at me. I'm pissed as hell at me." Mike threw up his hands.

"I won't lie and say that I'm completely comfortable with it, but that's because it's all new. I trust her with you. I know that you would do anything to keep her safe. That's what's important to me."

"Well, hell." Mike ran a hand through his hair, smearing deer blood through it.

"How did she react?" Cayden asked.

"She was shocked, but she didn't slap my face or burst into tears."

"How did you react?"

Mike shook his head. "I ran outside in my sock feet without my coat or gloves."

Cayden chuckled. "I'd say there's some attraction on her side, as well, then. I know she's been checking you out some when you weren't looking."

"This is all kinds of messed up. You know that, right?" Mike asked.

"Probably, but nothing is like it used to be before all the disasters. All that matters to me is that Nancy is happy and safe. I know you can help keep her safe. I believe you can help me keep her happy, as well."

"What if she doesn't want anything to do with me?" Mike asked.

"I don't think that's going to be an issue. Like I said, she's been checking you out when you haven't been looking. She's curious if nothing else, and now that you've kissed her, she's going to be even more curious."

"You need to talk to her, man. I don't want her to feel guilty about what happened. I kissed her. It wasn't the other way around. It just sort of happened."

Cayden nodded. "I'll talk to her while you're cleaning up. Give us some privacy for a couple of hours."

"I can do that. I'm going to need a damn bath after this. I've managed to get deer blood all over me." Mike said.

Cayden chuckled. "Yeah, your hair is sticking up with it."

They finished cutting up the deer and secured the meat, minus what they'd need for that night, in the cold box. Then Mike carted the remainder of the carcass deep into the woods to dispel any predators from hanging around the house. Cayden washed up the knives and pans they'd used then seasoned the meat and added water before settling it over the fire to cook.

"That took you a while," Nancy said when he'd plopped down on the couch next to her.

"Got a good bit of meat cut up. How are you doing?" he asked, searching her face.

She looked away. "Good. I'm glad you're back though."

"I'm sure glad to be back. This fire feels damn good right now." Cayden steered the conversation into safer territory. He didn't want to start anything until Mike was going to be conveniently out of pocket for an hour or two.

"I bet you got really cold waiting around for a deer to show up. Want me to add another piece of wood to the fire?" she asked.

"No. I can add it if I want it. I'm fine. Give me a hug, woman." Cayden pulled her into his arms.

He smiled when she snuggled next to him. He loved the feel of her against him. She fit perfectly in his embrace. The thought of seeing her in Mike's arms should have elicited hot shards of jealousy, but instead, it gave him a sense of relief. The last few months had shown him just how easily he could have lost his beloved Nancy. If sharing her with another man, with Mike, would lessen that chance, it would be worth it to him.

He buried his face in her hair and inhaled, marveling at the fresh scent of something citrusy. She smelled so damn good. He could sit there with her body pressed tightly against his forever. If only things were different.

But they aren't. I can't waste time thinking about what I wish. Nancy's safety and happiness is all that matters.

He adored her and prayed she would understand that things were just different out there and accept Mike as her other man. If she didn't, Cayden didn't know what he'd do. Everything hinged on her understanding and being attracted to the other man. He was banking on the knowledge that she'd been watching Mike with undisguised interest for the last few weeks. She obviously didn't realize he'd noticed. Finding out that he had was going to upset her.

He didn't want to do that, but there was nothing he could do to make it easier on her. She had to admit her attraction to the other man if he was going to get her to agree to welcome Mike into their relationship. Somehow he had a feeling she was going to fight him on that. How hard would determine if the three of them could make a go of it.

He prayed they could. For Nancy's sake. For all their sakes.

* * * *

Nancy sighed and leaned back against Cayden's chest as they relaxed before dinner was ready. Mike had decided to take a bath upstairs despite it being cold up there. He insisted that the hot water would warm up the bathroom and keep him comfortable enough.

"I've got to get this deer blood off me. I didn't realize I'd gotten it all in my hair," he'd said.

Thankfully all Cayden had needed to do was wash up in the kitchen sink. He'd fared much better than Mike for some reason even thought he'd had to field dress the deer before carrying it back to the house.

She snuggled deeper into his arms. She tried not to think about the kiss Mike had given her. It felt wrong to ponder it while lying in the arms of the man she considered her husband. What was wrong with her?

Nancy had to admit that the kiss had been electric despite the briefness of it. The moment he'd touched his lips to hers, she'd felt tiny sparks all through her bloodstream. That quick brush of his lips had been much more than an affectionate peck. It had been intense despite how quickly it had been over. Her body had reacted as if it had lasted minutes instead of seconds.

What is wrong with me? He isn't mine. He isn't Cayden. I shouldn't have reacted to him like I did. What am I going to tell Cayden? What if it happens again?

Well, it couldn't. She had to keep her distance from the other man. She'd been just as guilty as he'd been. She'd been teasing him. Yes, she had to admit, flirting with him. She'd thought it harmless, but evidently it hadn't been. Maybe there was no harmless flirting anymore. Times had changed. She needed to remember that.

"You feel good, honey," Cayden said, wrapping his arms around her from behind.

"You feel good, too."

"How was today while I was gone?"

She stiffened, then relaxed. She needed to tell him, but how?

"Good. Boring, mostly. It's too cold to go anywhere but in here," she told him.

Cayden was quiet for a long time. Then he surprised her.

"Mike told me what happened, Nancy."

Once again she stiffened and tried to pull away from him. Instead of letting her go, he turned her to look at him. Expecting to see anger or hurt burning in his eyes, she saw…was that relief?

"It's okay, hon."

"No, it's not okay. I cheated on you. Why aren't you furious with me?" she demanded.

"Because I was hoping you'd be attracted to him."

"What?"

"It's dangerous out here. I've almost lost you twice now. We need another man with us to keep you safe. I like Mike. He's strong, kind, and knows what life is like out here and we don't."

Nancy blinked at him. Was he suggesting what she thought he was? Did he expect her to accept the other man into their bed? Yeah, she knew that threesomes and even foursomes weren't all that uncommon out there, but Cayden and Mike together?

"You're saying you want Mike to be a part of our family?" she finally got out.

"Yes. You're obviously attracted to each other. I trust him with you, Nancy. I know he'd die to protect you just like I would. Maybe together that won't be necessary and you'd be safe." Cayden cupped her face in his warm hands. "The thought of losing you because I was too stubborn to admit that I can't take care of you out here scares the hell out of me, honey. Just think about it."

"I—I don't know if I can do what you're asking me, Cayden. I like Mike, but…"

She let that trail out. Nancy wasn't even sure she could put it into words. He was suggesting that she take Mike as a lover. That didn't sit well with her despite the sexual attraction she felt for the other man. Yeah, sparks flew when he touched her. Even when it was innocent like when their hands brushed. But have sex with him? What about Cayden? Where would he be when it happened?

Stop it. It's not going to happen. I can't possibly have sex with Mike when Cayden is my husband. It isn't right.

But a tendril of anticipation threaded its way into her mind at the thought. She was attracted to him, and obviously he was attracted to her from that kiss, but just because it had happened didn't mean he really liked her that way. When two people were cooped up together all the time like they had been, it was only natural something like that might happen. Right?

"All I'm asking is that you keep an open mind and think about it for now, Nancy. He obviously cares about you. I think it could be more if you gave him a chance."

"I don't know what to say, Cayden. You're asking me to have sex with another man besides you. Don't you think that's a little weird?" she asked.

His brows furrowed. "I know it sounds that way, but everything is different out here. The world is a different place. Don't think about it as cheating or whatever. Think of it as having a bigger family where you feel safe and cared for. You know I love you, Nancy. I'd do anything for you and that includes sharing you with another man if it will make you safer."

Nancy searched his eyes and saw the truth of that in his eyes. He was serious. Very serious. He wanted her to accept Mike into their lives. Why did that send a thrill of excitement along her spine? It shouldn't, but it did.

She wrapped her arms around herself and turned to look into the flames of the fire. Without saying anything else, she got up and poked at the meat swimming in the now bubbling gravy. Dinner would be ready before long. Mike would be downstairs again soon. How could she look him in the eyes with this new knowledge swimming around in her head like sharks circling prey?

"Nancy?"

"I don't know, Cayden. I just don't know if I can do that. I need time."

"We've got until spring. Then we have to look for another place to live if you can't accept Mike."

"No pressure," she joked.

"I'm sorry. I'm so sorry that I can't take care of you on my own, but I can't, honey."

Nancy turned back around to face Cayden. "I love you. You know that, don't you?"

"I know you do. Nothing will ever make me think otherwise. Welcoming Mike into our bed won't change how I feel about you either," he said.

Nancy shivered then walked over to sit on the couch next to him once again. How would Mike feel about Cayden? How would she feel about Mike? There were so many unanswered questions in her head that she couldn't concentrate on any one at the moment. She needed time to puzzle it all out in her mind before she could even think about making a decision.

The sound of footfalls on the stairs jerked her back from the carousel of thoughts circling in her mind. A tingling of awareness and anticipation thrilled across her skin like tiny biting ants at the thought of him in the same room with them. Her newfound knowledge had her hyper-aware of him now.

"Feel better?" Cayden asked the other man as he stood in front of the fireplace warming his hands.

"I will once I've warmed back up again," he said.

"I imagine it got pretty cold up there despite the hot water," Nancy ventured.

"Yeah. But having a bath felt damn good. I'll be glad when winter is over," Mike said.

"Except that when it is, we'll be leaving," Nancy said.

To her surprise, Mike shook his head. "You don't have to go. There's plenty of room here for you to stay."

Nancy jerked her head toward Cayden. The other man's eyes widened at the offer, but he didn't say anything.

"You wouldn't mind?" she asked.

"No. I like having the two of you around. We can enlarge the garden to accommodate the three of us. I'd miss you when you were gone. It's lonely here all by myself even with my sister and her family only thirty minutes away."

"We'd be a family if the three of us stuck together," Cayden said.

"That's up to Nancy. I'm not pushing her into anything she isn't comfortable with. I'd like to be a family, but you can't ask her to feel something she doesn't," Mike said.

"I'm not. If she doesn't care about you enough to give this a try then we won't," Cayden said.

Nancy walked across the room to stare out the window. She curled her arms around herself in an effort to fend off the chill being away from the fire caused. Could she give the three of them a chance? Could she give Mike a chance?

Chapter Eight

Nancy jumped every time Mike walked near her. She wasn't afraid of him, only super aware of him now that everything had been brought out into the open. Knowing that he wanted to be with her, make love with her, had her nerves as jumpy as grasshoppers in the warm summer sun. She couldn't stop staring at him when she thought he wasn't looking. She was sure Cayden noticed her preoccupation with the other man, and that worried her, as well.

Would he think she was more interested in Mike than him now?

I'm going to drive myself crazy if I keep second guessing everything. Cayden thinks it will work and it's worked for other families. I just need to stop obsessing over it and let things happen naturally.

Whatever naturally was. Nancy wasn't sure how things were supposed to go. She'd never been around a true threesome before to know.

It had been three days since they'd talked about the possibilities. For three days she'd been coiled up tighter than a clock spring. Something had to give. She was going to explode if it didn't.

They'd just finished breakfast when Cayden stood to carry his plate to the kitchen.

"I'm going to milk the cow and feed the chickens. I'll be back in a little while," he said.

"I can do that. You took care of them yesterday," Mike said.

"Nah. I'm getting stir crazy sitting around inside. You can take them tonight." Cayden strode from the room.

Mike thrust his hands on his hips and shook his head. “I could have done it.”

“Cayden never could sit still. He’s used to working more than he has here. There was always something needing to be done back at the commune,” Nancy explained.

“Come spring it will be that way here. Digging up the garden and planting it will take from sun up to sun down, then there’s keeping it weeded and watered,” Mike said.

“We’ll all be busy.”

“All day every day.”

Mike sat next to her on the couch so close she could feel his body heat. Their thighs nearly brushed as he bent forward and rested his elbows on his knees. Nancy was hyper-aware of him now. He hadn’t shaved since she and Cayden had arrived and now had a light brown beard that she ached to comb with her fingers. His sandy brown hair lay disheveled from running his hands through it all morning.

Nancy could admit she was attracted to him now, but worried that it wouldn’t be enough for her to handle anything physical with Cayden’s image in her head. That might change over time if she gave them a chance, but she was afraid it was too soon.

Evidently Mike didn’t think it was because he chose that moment to lay a hand on her thigh. She jerked her head toward him, eyes wide.

“Easy, Nancy. I’m not going to attack you.”

“Y—you just startled me,” she said.

“I feel like we’ve been tiptoeing around each other for weeks now instead of days. If my touch upsets you this much, we aren’t going to be able to do this.” He started to remove his hand.

Nancy covered his with her own. “I’m sorry. I’m just on edge. That’s all.”

His warm hand seemed to sear her skin through the material of her jeans. It felt good there. She could admit that to herself. She liked him touching her. Was that wrong? She hoped not. Thought that it wasn’t since the entire goal was for her to accept Mike into her and Cayden's life. Into their bed.

He squeezed her thigh then removed his hand to wrap his arm around her shoulders from behind. It felt odd at first, but as she relaxed into his embrace, Nancy admitted that it felt nice. She and Cayden hadn't been intimate since they'd ended up at Mike's house. There wasn't any privacy with them living on top of one another like they were.

Yes, they'd hugged, kissed and held hands, but nothing more. Now she was sitting there in front of the fire with Mike's arm around her shoulders and enjoying it. When he pulled her tighter against his side, she finally allowed herself to lean into him. It felt good. Better than good. It felt…right. He felt right. She wasn't sure why, but Nancy liked Mike and having him hold her didn't feel as foreign as she'd expected.

"I love your hair, Nancy. Like how it curls around your face and down your back." He lifted his other hand to tug on one of her curls. He looped it behind her ear then bent over. She felt his lips against her cheek as he kissed her there. Then he trailed kisses down her cheek to her jaw and back around to just below her ear.

She shivered at the touch of his soft, full lips. Her pulse picked up as her heart pounded a hard rhythm in her chest. His mouth on her was amazing and scary all at the same time. She knew this was what Cayden had wanted, but it still felt naughty to have him kissing her.

"Relax. I'm not going to jump on you. Just let things go as they will. Don't think so hard about it." Cayden's warm breath brushed her ear as he spoke.

"I can't help it. I know we've talked about it, but this is real."

"I know."

He sucked on her earlobe then mouthed his way down her neck until he reached the collar of her shirt. Mike nudged it aside and nipped at her shoulder before lifting his head and tilting her chin toward him with one finger. His hazel eyes seemed overly bright as he slowly lowered his head to capture her lips in a kiss.

It started out soft like butterflies lighting on a flower then grew more insistent as he cupped her cheek in his hand. Nancy admitted that the kiss stirred feelings inside of her she hadn't wanted to admit were there. It opened up emotions that threatened to drown her as he deepened the kiss, running the tip of his tongue over her lower lip, burning her like fire racing through a forest.

She opened to him, hardly aware of what she was doing until his tongue slid alongside hers in a sensual dance she hadn't expected to like. He teased and explored as she moaned with pleasure before she realized it. The kiss warmed her from the inside out. She hadn't expected it to be this good. An inkling of worry pierced her heart, but before she could act on it, he withdrew, nipping at her lower lip as he did.

"You taste like apples and cinnamon," he said in a hoarse voice. "Please don't tell me you didn't like that."

Nancy had to clear her voice in order to speak. "I would be lying if I did. I didn't expect to like it, but I did."

"Thank you for your honesty, Nancy."

"I'm not going to lie to you, Mike. I liked kissing you, but I'm still a little nervous about hurting Cayden."

"That's to be expected, but he's the one who suggested it and seems okay as much as he can be. I'm sure he will have to deal with it when we're all three together, but it's just you and me right now. Just the two of us." Mike brushed her hair back again and leaned down to reclaim her mouth with his.

Nancy participated this time. She curled her tongue around his as they moved and rolled over each other in the kiss. Mike pulled her closer to him, pressing her body against his as his mouth moved on hers. The closeness felt good. Right. She could admit it to herself now. She was more than a little attracted to him. She wanted to feel his hands on her bare skin and though that should have worried her, with his mouth exploring hers, it didn't in that moment.

Mike withdrew and leaned his head against hers. "Damn, you go to my head, Nancy. I want to feel your body against mine."

"I was thinking the same thing," she admitted as her breath came in quick pants.

"Can I touch you?" he asked.

"You are touching me."

"I want to explore your body, sweetness. I want to feel how your full breasts fill my hands. I want to touch them and lick them. Will you let me?" he asked.

She gazed into his warm hazel eyes, bright with arousal even as heavy lids spoke volumes as to how he felt. Nancy didn't want to deny him. Couldn't deny him in that moment. Thoughts of Cayden were buried deep as she nodded without a sound.

He didn't wait for her to change her mind. Mike began unbuttoning the flannel shirt she was wearing and exposed her heavy breasts. Nancy's nipples were hard against the lacy material of her bra. One touch of Mike's fingers across the taut peaks had her moaning and shifting restlessly against his body.

"Does that feel good, sweetness?" he asked.

"You know it does."

He dipped his head and licked and kissed all across the exposed part of her chest, sliding his tongue beneath the edges of her bra. Then he lowered his head further and sucked on her nipples through the satin exterior of the material covering her.

Fire raced through her body. Perhaps it was partly because of the fact that she'd belonged to Cayden alone for so long or maybe it was just because it felt that good, but Nancy had never gotten so aroused so quickly with only some light touching before. She reached up and wrapped one hand around Mike's neck, urging him to continue his exploration.

He didn't need any further urging. Mike slid one hand into the front of her bra and caressed her aching breast. He lightly pinched her tingling nipple. It only added to the heat beginning between her legs. Her pussy was growing wet and needy. It wasn't Cayden, but still she was hot with desire.

On some level, Nancy felt like she should be appalled at what was happening to her body, but she knew this was what Cayden wanted in order to better protect her. She just prayed he wouldn't change his mind after she'd dropped her guard around Mike and let him in. That would devastate her.

"You're so responsive, so amazing, Nancy."

"You make me feel so good."

He tugged her bra up so that the lacy cups lay above her exposed breasts where he could see her exposed breasts, touch them, taste them. He lowered his head and sucked on one hard tip, teasing it with his tongue as he sucked in more of her breast. His other hand molded her flesh with his fingers, squeezing then pinching at her nipple as he sucked hard on her other breast. Nancy felt as if her body was on fire. Blood raced through her veins, hard and hot. Her breath came in short gasps as her pussy tightened with each tug at her nipple.

"Mike."

"I've got you, Nancy."

He lowered one hand to unbutton then lower the zipper of her jeans. Before she knew what he intended, he'd slid his hand into her pants and located her pussy with his fingers. She cried out when he began slowly rubbing over her clit. The dual sensations of her breasts being loved and her clit being stimulated had her on a collision course with an orgasm faster than she would have thought possible.

"Please don't stop," she begged as she bucked against his hands.

"I won't. Come for me, Nancy. I want to feel you come apart in my hands."

He returned to tormenting her breasts with his mouth and the fingers of his other hand. Everything felt too much, too good.

"So good. Can't believe this is happening," she managed to get out.

"No more thinking, sweetness. Just feel."

He drove her crazy with his hot mouth and talented fingers until she was sure she'd explode with the pressure building inside of her. He thrust a finger inside her hot, wet cunt, all the while teasing her clit with his thumb. His draws on her breast mimicked what his finger was doing inside her pussy. The combination was driving her ever closer to that elusive climax she was sure she'd die from.

Finally, when she thought she'd pass out with the need to come, he pinched her clit as he nipped at one nipple and everything went hot, blinding white as Nancy exploded with the orgasm. She cried out in ecstasy.

"Mike."

He stroked her down from the high she rode until all that was left was the ringing in her ears and the warm pleasure that enveloped her after the throes of coming slowly seeped away.

Nancy started to doubt what she'd done, but Mike seemed to know what she was thinking. He kissed her softly while he repositioned her breasts inside her bra.

"No doubts, sweetness. We did nothing wrong." He buttoned up her shirt then refastened and zipped her jeans. "Cayden knows we're going to be experimenting some to see if there's any chemistry between us. I'd say that was a yes. What about you?" he asked.

She felt shy and uncomfortable now. "I guess. I mean that was great, but you didn't, um…"

He chuckled. "Come? I can wait until you're ready. It's not time for anything more yet."

"It was good, Mike. I'm just afraid that Cayden will change his mind. Then I'll feel even worse."

"He's not going to change his mind. Believe me. I've talked to him enough to know he's determined for us to become a family. He wants you safe and we're friends. He just hopes that you'll be amenable to the idea and maybe come to care about me like you love him."

"I do care about you, Mike. You've been nothing but good to us from the first day."

"I'm glad that damn mutt howled at my door that night," he said.

"Galahad must have gone out with Cayden. Normally he's in front of the fire." Nancy looked around. "I'm glad it was you he found."

"Me, too."

Nancy shifted on the couch. She finally lowered her hand to Mike's, though, where it rested next to her own. He pulled her closer with an arm around her shoulders. It felt good to be enveloped by him. The warm fire and his hot body kept her from thinking overly much about what they'd done.

Until the back door opened then closed.

Chapter Nine

Nancy started to pull away from Mike, but he stopped her. His face held no guilt, only resolve. She realized he wanted to prove to her that Cayden was fine with their getting to know each other. She stilled in his arms and waited with a knot in the bottom of her stomach.

Cayden joined them several minutes later in the living room. His eyes took them in and a quiet smile softened his face as he huddled up in front of the fire. Galahad pranced into the room and lay down in front of the roaring flames, as well.

"I'll be glad when spring gets here. I'm sick of freezing my balls off every time I go outside," Cayden said.

"You took the warmer part of the day. It'll be colder than that when I go out tonight to see about the animals," Mike said.

Cayden chuckled. "Can't say I'm not smart."

Nancy sighed. Cayden acted as if nothing was amiss. Maybe he truly was okay with her and Mike becoming intimate. He wasn't acting uncomfortable at the sight of the two of them sitting so close together with Mike's arm around her shoulders. It both relieved her and hurt, if she were to be honest with herself.

Once he'd warmed up, Cayden sat on the other side of her, close enough that their thighs touched, as well. She felt completely surrounded by the two men. It wasn't unpleasant. She liked having them both blanketing her. She felt cared for and safe.

Still, what she and Mike had done had her gut clenching with Cayden so close now. She worried he'd figure it out and be angry, but the longer they sat there talking, the less she worried. Finally, Nancy relaxed and listened to the men talk, letting the anxiety ease from her body.

The two men talked about the animals and how the cow was antsy the last few days they'd been out to milk her. Mike suggested that there might be wolves sneaking around and that they should watch for tracks. They couldn't afford to have a pack of them hanging around.

Then talk turned to spring and what all would need to be done once the ground was no longer frozen. She sank back onto the couch and listened as they made plans and enjoyed the knowledge that everything was okay between them. She'd worried when she'd heard the door open with Cayden's return. Now she didn't feel as anxious about it all. What did that say about her? She wasn't sure.

"What do you think, Nancy?" Mike asked.

"I'm sorry. I guess I wasn't listening."

"We thought we'd plant an herb garden separate from the main garden this year. It would make it easier for you to get what you need without having to climb around in the rest of it," he said.

"That would be great. Do you have seeds for the herbs?" she asked.

"Yeah. Not as many as I'd like, but we can make do and save more seeds for the next garden," Mike said.

"You're going to be busy when the harvest comes in," Cayden said.

"I know. It was like that at the commune. I'll be fine. Hopefully we can put up enough food for all of us," she said.

Mike stood. "I'm going to warm us up some stew."

Nancy watched him walk into the kitchen to pull out the stew before bringing it back into the living room to set over the fire. She was hungry. It surprised her that she hadn't realized it before now. Truly she'd been so caught up in what had happened between her and Mike that she hadn't even realized that she was starving.

"That smells good," Cayden said. "I got hungry out there."

"Should be warm enough to eat in a little while," Mike assured them.

They continued talking about the upcoming spring then ate the delicious stew before relaxing and dozing together on the couch.

Nancy slowly became aware of the feel of a warm hand against her bare belly. She opened her eyes to find Cayden smiling at her. His warm brown eyes held a hint of mischief as he moved his hand farther up her belly beneath her shirt.

"Mike's gone to see about the animals and check the traps he set. It's been a long time since we've made love, hon."

Just like that, need spiraled inside though worry about the other man walking in on them cooled the feeling somewhat. Cayden's hand closed over one breast and that need won out. She arched into his hand and moaned.

"I want to see you, Nancy. I want to see how your blush as I make you come covers your chest and neck. I love that I can make you do that."

Nancy could only nod. She wanted to see him, as well. Even as he began unbuttoning her shirt, she struggled to do the same to him. Finally he brushed her hands aside and removed hers before doing the same to his. Then he pulled the undershirt over his head before unsnapping her bra and drawing the lacy scrap of clothing down her arms and off to land on top of their discarded clothes next to the couch.

"God, you're beautiful." He fingered her nipples then lowered his head and took one into his mouth while pinching and pulling on the other one.

Nancy moaned again and held his head to her breasts, splaying her hand in his hair before tugging on it as she grew more restless. She wanted him and they didn't have a lot of time. The last thing she wanted was for Mike to walk in on them while they were having sex. Somehow that seemed wrong after he'd brought her to orgasm while forgoing it himself.

"Please, Cayden. I need you," she said with a groan.

He seemed to understand her urgency and slid to his knees beside the sofa to unfasten her jeans and pull them over her hips when she arched off the couch, then down her legs. He left her socks on. Then he unfastened his own jeans and pulled them off, along with his boxers, as well.

The sight of his masculine body with the tight muscles across his arms and shoulders and the way his chest held just a little hair between his nipples made her pussy even wetter than before. She loved looking at him. From his amazing brown eyes along with his chiseled features to his amazing body. She allowed her eyes to dip lower to see the heavy arousal of his cock as it stood against his abdomen.

His eyelids seemed to droop with her perusal of his dick. He splayed his hand across her belly before gently spreading her legs and running his fingers through the hair above her pussy. He tugged on it then circled her clit with his thumb. Nancy threw her head back at the sudden touch.

"So good," she managed to breathe out.

"I love how responsive you are, Nancy. I love that I can just touch you and you're hot and wet and ready for me."

As if to prove it, Cayden entered her with two fingers, filling her pussy with them as he pumped them in and out in a slow, sensual movement that had her arching her back to meet each thrust.

"Please, Cayden. I need you. It's been so long."

"Easy, hon. I want this to last and it won't when I get inside of you. I'm already a second away from coming just looking at you and feeling your tight pussy sucking at my fingers."

Nancy thrashed her head from side to side as pleasure built with each thrust of his fingers and every touch of his thumb at her clit. He suddenly removed his fingers and climbed on the couch, kneeling over her as he drew one of her legs over his arm and fitted his hard dick at her entrance.

"I can't wait any longer. I'm sorry, hon. I promise I'll go slower next time."

"I don't care, Cayden. I want you so much. I can't wait either." Nancy reached up and grasped his upper arms, pulling him toward her.

She gasped when he pressed forward, entering her with the tip of his shaft before pulling back and repeating the movement until he was able to surge forward and fill her with his thick dick. She groaned out loud at the delicious feeling of him finally filling her. She'd dreamed of this for weeks. It had been so long since they'd been together that she'd begun to fantasize about it all the time.

"Fuck, you're tight. I'm never going to last, hon."

"Take me, Cayden. I can't stand it."

He bent down and kissed her, a hard desperate kiss that left her breathless. Then he began thrusting in earnest. Pulling out then tunneling in once again. Over and over he filled her cunt with his hard cock, rasping over that sweet spot that left her dizzy with pleasure. She could feel her climax just out of reach and arched her back each time he filled her.

As if knowing how close she was, Cayden reached between them and rubbed his thumb across her clit until she exploded with pleasure that had built up so quickly she was almost dizzy with it as it all crashed down around her.

"Fuck! You're squeezing my dick like a vise, Nancy." Then he squeezed his eyes shut and followed her over, giving in to his own orgasm.

It felt like hours before she was able to open her eyes and breathe normally again. Cayden had collapsed so that his head rested on her chest. His heavy breathing slowly evened out, as well.

"I missed that," he said. "Not just the climax, but just being inside of you. With you."

"I missed it, too," she admitted.

Cayden slowly pulled out then sat, pulling her legs onto his lap. "You look so pretty in the firelight. I like seeing you naked with that flush on your cheeks."

She felt the heat of a blush crawl up her neck and into her cheeks. How could she blush when they'd been lovers for nearly two years now?

He chuckled. "We'd better get dressed. Although I'm hoping you will choose to let Mike into our family, I don't think it's fair for him to walk in and find us like this."

That spurred Nancy into jumping up, nearly kicking Cayden in his crotch in the process.

"Whoa. Careful there. You don't have to get in such a hurry, hon," Cayden said.

Nancy slid into her panties and jeans then struggled with her bra until Cayden brushed her hands aside and fastened it for her. She could feel the fine tremors in her hands as she manipulated the buttons into the holes of her shirt. Only when she felt completely dressed did she begin to calm down. Cayden pulled her close to him.

"Relax, Nancy. He knows we're a couple, and we didn't do anything wrong. You act like we're teenagers who nearly got caught necking on your parents' couch," he teased.

She smiled up at him, allowing the anxiety to slowly leech away. "I can't help it. I feel like a teenager. We just made love on the couch in Mike's house."

"You shouldn't feel guilty, hon. There's no need."

"He doesn't have a woman, Cayden. That can't be fair to him that we have sex and he can't."

"He could have a woman," he said in a quiet voice.

"Cayden. I…" She wasn't sure what she would have said because the kitchen door opened then closed and all the worry she'd nearly put behind her roared back to swamp her in nerves once again.

* * * *

"I'm back. Got a rabbit, believe it or not," Mike called out.

"I'll see about the milk," Nancy said, jumping up.

Cayden stood, as well, and followed her into the kitchen. He could tell that Nancy was back to being nervous as she rushed into the kitchen. He frowned. This was never going to work if she continued to fight her feelings. He knew she was attracted to the other man by the quick looks at him when she didn't think either of them noticed.

Am I expecting too much? What if she never agrees to letting Mike in? We can't live here under his roof as a couple. That would be asking a lot of the other man.

Cayden sighed. There was nothing he could do to push her onto Mike. He would encourage her and pray she finally let him into their lives. It wasn't fair, but he needed the other man's help to take care of her. Somehow he had to get them together without damaging his and Nancy's relationship in the process.

"Looks like a nice size rabbit," he commented when he'd joined the other man in the kitchen.

"Should make a good meal for us. Rabbit stew will be a nice change from the deer," Mike said.

"I could fry it if you'd rather have something different," Nancy said as she took care of the milk.

"How about frying it then making gravy and having it that way?" Mike suggested.

"That sounds even better," Cayden agreed.

He watched as Nancy flitted around gathering what she'd need to fry up the rabbit meat then make gravy with it. She carried the heavy skillet into the living room, followed by Mike. He'd just walked in behind them to see Mike sniff the air then close his eyes. The other man knew they'd made love. He just prayed Nancy wouldn't notice. It would embarrass her so much to realize he could smell the sex in the air.

Thankfully, she was so busy getting ready to cook the rabbit that she missed the longing in Mike's eyes as he stared at her. He handed her the bowl with the cut up rabbit meat then stepped back out of the way as she got to work.

"Any tracks around the yard to indicate a wolf or wolf pack?" Cayden asked.

"No. Not sure what had the cow so anxious the other night. There hasn't been any more snow, so the tracks wouldn't have been covered up."

"How did Galahad act when you were out checking the traps?" he asked.

Mike shrugged. "He romped and played in the snow like a kid. Didn't seem to sense anything that upset him."

"Think he'd pick up on a predator close by?" Cayden asked.

"I think so. He seems to be pretty protective of us. Or at least of Nancy."

Speaking of the dog, Galahad walked over and leaned against Cayden, looking up at him as if to say, *Pet me, human. I need your affection.*

Cayden laughed and petted the huge dog. He sighed and walked over to lie down near Nancy as she tended to the meat. When he Cayden thought about just how close they'd come to freezing to death, all he could think about was making sure that damn dog was well cared for. He'd saved their lives.

"I'm going to pull in some more wood while we wait on dinner," Mike said.

"I'll help." Cayden walked after the other man into the kitchen. "It will go faster if we both do it."

"Not going to complain. It's still cold as shit out there." Mike pulled on his boots then his coat and gloves.

Cayden followed suit and joined the other man outside at the wood pile they had stacked between two trees. They each carted wood to the back porch. After a few minutes, Mike spoke up.

"I managed to make a little headway with Nancy earlier while you were out taking care of the animals this morning. She isn't immune to me at least, but I'm still not sure this is going to work."

"It has to. The more I think about living somewhere alone with her and not being able to be with her all the time, the sicker I feel inside. I have to be able to hunt and work the garden when she's not right beside me. That scares the crap out of me."

Mike sighed. "I'm trying, but I don't want to make her feel pressured into anything."

"Just keep doing whatever you're doing and she'll get more accustomed to your touch and relax more around you."

"I, um, made her come this morning." Mike didn't look at him as he picked up another load of wood.

Cayden felt his heart slam into his rib cage. He hadn't realized the other man had made that much headway. Part of him was happy, while another part of him felt betrayed. He had to banish that thought, bury it deep. This was about making sure Nancy was safe. He couldn't allow his own feelings to overshadow that.

"That's good. That's very good," he said instead.

"I know you made love with her while I was gone. She didn't act nervous about it, did she?" Mike asked.

"No. I wouldn't have known that you'd been able to do that if you hadn't told me. It isn't affecting our relationship, if that's what you're worried about." Cayden dropped the wood on the pile then brushed off his hands. "Think this is enough for now?"

"Yeah. Dinner should be ready by now anyway."

Cayden followed Mike inside and turned the knowledge of Mike with Nancy over in his head as he removed his boots, coat, and gloves. The other man had seemed hesitant about admitting that he'd been intimate with Nancy. It was up to Cayden to soothe the other man's fears of cheating with Nancy. He wasn't sure how he was going to do that, but he had to try. Everything hinged on both he and Nancy overcoming the guilt and relaxing around him despite the two of them having sex together. Part of that process depended on him getting used to the idea and not letting his jealousy fester. He had to get past it and move on. It was the only way to make sure Nancy was safe.

Chapter Ten

Mike stretched before getting out of the recliner and standing. He would be happy as hell when spring got there so that he could sleep in a bed again. The damn recliner was comfortable enough for an afternoon nap, but didn't even come close to what it felt like to sleep in a bed. He stretched again.

It was early, the sun had barely begun to rise. He decided he'd tend to the animals before Cayden and Nancy woke. No need for them to get up early if they didn't have to. He peeked at them on the pallet in front of the fire and smiled. Nancy lay on her side with Cayden spooned tightly against her, his arm thrown over her waist with the covers drawn up under Nancy's chin.

Damn, he wanted to be on her other side with her arm thrown over him. He wished she were more receptive, but he understood that this was something major to be springing on her. Especially after what she'd run from in the first place. Despite it only being one man she would be expected to welcome into her bed, it was still foreign to her. He could appreciate that.

Mike pulled on his boots, coat, and gloves then opened the door to the cold, early April morning. Another few weeks and the snow would be gone and the warmer air of spring would blow. They'd have to work fast to get the garden dug up and ready to plant. The growing season was short there. Where the southern areas would be able to plant in late March, they'd have to hope to get their seeds in the ground by late April or early May.

Mike tended to the chickens, gathering eggs and feeding them, then turned to the dairy cow.

"Morning, Meg. How about being nice to me this morning and let me milk you without a fuss."

Mike settled on the stool and began milking the cow. She mooed at him a couple of times, but didn't shift around like she sometimes did. He thanked the good Lord she was behaving this morning. He really didn't want to get milk all over his hands or waste it on the ground.

Twenty minutes later, after tending to feeding the cow and carrying the milk and eggs inside, he once again removed his outer clothes and set about straining the milk and putting it away.

"Morning." Nancy gave him a shy smile as she pattered into the kitchen in her sock feet.

"Morning, Nancy. Did you sleep well?" he asked.

"Yeah, but I'll be glad when I can sleep on an actual bed again."

He chuckled. "I was just thinking the same thing when I got up this morning."

"I bet sleeping in that recliner isn't all that comfortable. I'm sorry you didn't get the floor." She cocked her head. "Or maybe not. The chair might be more comfortable than the floor."

"I think they both have their negatives. Is Cayden still sleeping?"

"Yeah, I don't think he fell asleep as fast as I did. I woke up to go to the bathroom and he was still awake."

"Something bothering him?" he asked.

"I don't think so. He didn't say if it was."

He watched as she washed her hands then gathered up the eggs. Mike couldn't take his eyes off of her. She was beautiful, with her tousled black hair and those dark mysterious eyes. He loved that she had wide sensuous hips with a narrow waist and rounded belly. She was just the sort of woman he'd always been attracted to.

Before he could second guess himself, he took the bowl of eggs from her and pulled her into his arms for a kiss. He couldn't help himself. He needed a kiss like he needed his next meal.

Mike pressed his lips against hers, then nibbled her lower lip. She parted hers and he dove in to explore her mouth with his tongue, teasing and touching every part of her that he could reach. She hesitated then joined him in the kiss, slanting her mouth so that she could explore more of his, as well.

He felt her relax into his embrace. It went a long way toward making him feel like she was beginning to accept him. When she moaned, Mike reveled in the fact that he'd done that. He'd given her pleasure and she was accepting it. He pulled back just enough to suck on her lower lip before slowly releasing her.

Suddenly she stiffened then pulled away with a gasp. He looked up to see her eyes focused on something behind him. He turned around and wrapped an arm around Nancy's waist just as he became aware of Cayden standing in the doorway with his arms crossed, leaning against the doorjamb.

"Cayden. I…" Nancy began.

"It's okay, Nancy. I told you I was okay with this." Cayden smiled at her but Mike could see something more in the man's eyes. Was it hurt?

"This isn't right. I don't know why I let that happen," Nancy said with tears in her voice.

Mike pulled her tighter against his side. "You don't have anything to feel guilty about. I seduced you into kissing me, sweetness."

At the same time, Cayden pushed off from the doorway and stood in front of her, cupping her cheeks in his hands.

"It's okay, honey. This is what we all need. I'm okay with this. You did nothing wrong." Cayden kissed her lightly on the lips then pulled her from Mike's arms to envelop her in a hug.

Mike relaxed a little, knowing that Cayden wasn't going to make Nancy feel bad about kissing him. He'd thought for a few seconds that he'd do just that.

"I don't know about you guys, but I'm starving. How about fried eggs?" Cayden asked.

Nancy smiled through tears she hadn't allowed to fall. "I can handle that."

The next few hours were taken up with breakfast, cleaning up afterward, and talking about when the snow would melt.

"The wind felt a little more southerly while I was out this morning. That will bring warmer weather soon," Mike told them.

"I can't wait to be able to sit outside without wearing so many clothes to keep warm," Nancy said.

"I can't wait until I don't freeze my ass off every time Galahad needs to go out," Cayden admitted.

"He can't help it. He has to go when he has to go. We have a nice warm bathroom to use." Nancy poked Cayden in the ribs.

"Hey." Cayden rubbed his side with a grin.

Mike liked seeing Nancy so relaxed and was glad the earlier kiss hadn't changed that. It gave him hope that they did have a future together. The three of them. He wanted more than ever to be a part of their family. If that didn't happen, Mike wasn't sure what he would do.

* * * *

Nancy sighed and sat down on the couch next to Cayden. She'd cleaned up the dinner dishes and was glad to be off her feet again. Winter had made her lazy. She couldn't imagine how she'd do once spring and summer arrived. That would be a slap in the face for sure. She smiled. It didn't matter. They had a home there with Mike. She knew the other man wanted them to stay and Cayden was convinced the three of them could be a family. She hoped he was right, but couldn't help but feel apprehensive about becoming intimate with the other man.

Mike walked into the room, carrying another log for the fire. He dropped it in the fireplace then used the poker to settle it where he wanted it before putting down the poker and sitting on the couch on the other side of her. Right on the other side of her. Close enough that their thighs touched.

Nancy was aware of every place they touched. His shoulder brushed hers, as well. He crossed his arms and stared into the flames that danced in the fireplace. Nancy couldn't help but stiffen up at the sudden contact, but slowly found herself relaxing between the two men. Cayden held her hand and brought it to his lips where he kissed her knuckles before lowering their joined fingers to his lap.

"I like this," Mike said.

"What?" Nancy asked in a pinched voice.

"Sitting here with the two of you enjoying the peace and quiet and a roaring fire. It's nice."

"You left out Galahad," she teased.

"Yeah, he looks good stretched out in front of the fire. He's about as big as a lion skin rug would be."

The big dog lifted his head and yawned then lowered it back to rest on his paws. Nancy laughed. He was a big cumbersome thing when he raced outside in the snow, pushing through it and rolling around like a six year old.

"I know he's warm to my feet," Nancy said, brushing her socked feet over Galahad's back.

Mike uncrossed his arms and rested his hand on her thigh. Nancy stiffened then made herself relax. She wasn't sure if Cayden had noticed or not. If he had, he didn't react to it. She waited for him to, but all she felt was him squeezing her hand briefly. She looked up, and seeing a smile, knew he was okay with Mike's hand on her.

Again mixed feelings warred within her. She wanted Mike's touch but also wanted Cayden to object to it. That was so messed up. She leaned into Cayden then after hesitating, leaned against Mike, as well. His smile of encouragement sent shivers of heat down her back and over her chest.

"Comfortable?" Cayden asked out of the blue.

"Yes. It's warm between the two of you." She wasn't sure what to say.

"Good. I want you to be, hon."

For some reason, Nancy was almost positive that he wasn't talking about being comfortable sitting on the couch but sitting between him and Mike with Mike's hand on her thigh.

Nancy moved her other hand from her stomach and slowly reached over to rest her hand on top of Mike's hand where it lay casually on her leg. She felt him sigh and the slight squeeze he gave her thigh.

All of this was so new to her. She didn't know how to feel, what to do. Tension coiled inside her like a rattler waiting to strike. She kept expecting Cayden to say something, pull away from her or pull her away from Mike.

When that didn't happen, she gradually began to relax between them and smothered a sigh of relief. Cayden moved closer to her and kissed the side of her neck. He whispered in her ear how pretty she was in the firelight.

On her other side, Mike did the same. It felt strange to feel and hear the same things on either side of her. Mike's nose nuzzled behind her ear as Cayden kissed down her neck to nose aside her shirt and nip her collar bone.

Nancy shivered as Mike kissed her cheek then rubbed along her jaw with his mouth. So many sensations accosted her that she moaned without meaning to. It all felt so good and so bad at the same time. She'd never had two men shower attention on her at one time. Now, the kisses she'd shared with Mike didn't seem so scary anymore. Not when he was seducing her along with Cayden at the same time.

"You can't imagine how badly I want you, Nancy. Seeing you kiss and touch Cayden and knowing that you made love the other night when I was gone has me so hard right now I could pound nails with my dick. You do that to me." Mike's naughty words sent chills down her arms and had her pussy growing wetter than just their touch had already done.

"I—I don't know what to do. You're driving me crazy. Both of you," she finally got out.

Having both men touching and kissing her was more than her senses could process. She felt heat suffuse her chest and neck before rushing to her face. How could she get so turned on by two men? It didn't seem right, but she was.

Heat burned through her bloodstream at the feel of them caressing and loving her body. Their touch burned everywhere they went. Mike's hand on her thigh brushed closer to her center as Cayden's cupped one breast, brushing his thumb across her nipple until the peak was hard and aching. Suddenly her clothes felt cloying. She was hot and antsy. She needed out of her clothes.

"Please," she breathed.

"Please what, sweetness?" Mike asked.

"I'm so hot."

"I think she needs her clothes off," Cayden said.

"I'll take care of her pants if you'll work on her blouse," Mike said.

Together the two men worked to remove her clothes, leaving her completely naked between them. She wasn't really aware of it when their touch had her warmer than any clothes could possibly do for her. Nancy was on fire with need.

They continued their touching and kissing. Mike's fingers delved between her legs, teasing her pussy and clit with barely there touches that had her arching her hips in an effort to force his fingers to really touch her instead of lightly brushing across her.

Cayden molded one breast while he sucked on the nipple of the other one. The feel of his drawing on the tight bud went straight to her pussy, jumping up the pleasure to the point of pain. She needed more of their touches. She needed to come.

"Please. Mike, Cayden. I can't stand this." Nancy pulled at both of their shirts in an effort to get them to understand what she wanted. She wanted them naked like her, open for her touches.

Mike got the message first and pulled back to tug off his clothes while Cayden continued sucking and nipping her breasts. When Mike returned to her side, she gasped at the bright pink scars on his abdomen that marred their muscular appearance. She'd seen them before but they looked so much worse now for some reason.

"What happened to you?" she asked, jerking her eyes to his face.

"I was shot trying to protect my sister before she fell in love with her men," he said.

"It was just you and her?" she asked.

"Yeah, just the two of us and if her two men hadn't heard the gunshot while they were out riding their horses, they would have gotten her and killed me," he told her.

Nancy didn't know what to say to that. Cayden was right. She wasn't safe with just him to protect her. Then Mike drew her face toward him with one finger and kissed her. The heat of it burned as he thrust his tongue alongside hers, teasing and tempting her to tussle as he cupped her face in his large hands. She loved it. Loved the feel of his hands on her skin. Loved the knowledge that he truly wanted her as much as Cayden.

She felt it in his kiss. In the way he wrapped his hand around the back of her neck and held her to him. Nancy admitted to herself that she wanted him just as much as she wanted Cayden. It excited her and frightened her all at the same time. Even if it wasn't considered the norm out there in the wilds of the Border Lands, she knew she would still want him. That thought didn't worry her nearly as much as it should have.

Chapter Eleven

Mike couldn't believe he was finally touching Nancy the way he wanted to. She was bare to his touch and while Cayden removed his clothes, he cupped her breasts and flicked the nipples with his fingers. They were so tight. Perfect for sucking on. He loved her tits. They were just the right size for his hands and he had large hands. Mike bent down and drew one hard nipple into his mouth and sucked. She moaned for him. Not for Cayden, but for him. That went straight to his dick.

Her soft mewls tightened his balls and had his cock jerking at the sounds. He wanted her, but wanted her to be ready and as into the moment as he was. He continued suckling at her breast while he pulled and pinched at the other nipple.

When Cayden returned he relinquished his hold on her breasts and slid one hand down her belly to the soft thatch of curls at her pussy. He could already smell her heated arousal. They were stirring her desire with their touches and dirty words in her ears. Mike slid one finger through her folds to find her hot and wet. He wanted inside of her so badly he didn't know what to do.

"You're wet, baby. Do you want us?" he asked.

"Oh, God. I need you. I'm so hot," she breathed out.

He wasn't going to push her yet. He wanted this to be the beginning of their relationship. This first time he'd be happy to have her mouth on his hard cock. They had all the time in the world to move beyond that.

"I want to feel your mouth on my dick, babe. Can you suck me?" he asked, digging his fingers through her hair.

"Yes. I want to suck you, Mike." Her breathy reply had his shaft jerking once more.

"I'm going to take that pretty pussy, hon," Cayden told her.

They laid her on the couch so that Cayden could climb up with her and Mike could reach her mouth with his dick. She looked so pretty lying there with her eyes glazed with desire. She licked her lips, the sight almost more than he could handle. His dick was hard as steel with a bead of pre-cum leaking from the tip. He wanted her mouth on him like he wanted his next breath.

He watched Cayden lift her legs over his arms as he prepared to enter her. Her pussy glistened with her desire. He wanted to find out just how hot her tight wet cunt was for himself, but that would come later. For now he was content with having her hot little mouth on him, taking him to the back of her throat and sucking him dry.

He groaned at the sight of her taking Cayden's dick as he entered her. He went slow at first then pounded into her with his head thrown back. Mike knelt on the edge of the couch and touched his dick to the corner of Nancy's mouth.

"Suck me, babe. Let me feel that mouth on my cock."

Nancy opened and licked at the little drop at the top of his cock then licked all around the ridge then across the top before sucking him into her hot, wet mouth. She moaned around him, the vibrations streaking to his balls. Only a few sucks of her mouth and already his balls were boiling with the need to erupt. He'd never last with the way she sucked on him, taking him to the back of her throat with each draw. Mike groaned when she swallowed around him, the tight suction of her throat nearly making him shoot his load. Her mouth was dangerous.

He felt it when Nancy began to lose herself in Cayden's rhythm. The man was nearly there and taking Nancy with him. Mike pulled from her mouth in case she accidentally bit down when she came. He reached over and pulled on her nipples to help get her there. When she went over, she screamed and arched her back. Cayden bellowed and nearly collapsed over her as he came.

Mike waited as long as he could stand and tapped Nancy's mouth once she'd stopped panting from her orgasm.

"Suck me, babe."

He fed it to her when she opened and drew him in. She ran her tongue all along the thick vein then sucked him down. He gripped the base of his cock as he pumped himself in and out of her hot little mouth. Once again he grew close to emptying his load down her tight throat. When she took him all the way down and swallowed around him, his balls drew up tight against his body in an almost painful pinch.

"I'm going to come, babe. Swallow me down," he gritted out.

She sucked hard on him, swallowing like he asked when he came hard, shooting cum down her throat. He felt his ass cheeks cramp as he gave her everything he had. He swore as the last of the climax burned through him. He felt as if his toes had curled since they cramped, as well.

When he pulled free of her perfect little mouth, a drop of cum lay at the corner of her mouth. He reached down and scooped it up then held it to her mouth. She licked his finger clean and smiled up at him.

Yeah, she was happy with having him become part of her family. He had no doubt they'd have problems along the way, but this was a first step in sealing them together. To have someone to share the long hard work days of spring and summer and the long dark days of winter would be worth every bit of the pain of these first few months of getting things right between the three of them. He'd do his level best to make her happy. If she were happy, they'd all be happy.

Mike stood. "I'll go get a wet cloth to clean her up with, Cayden. Be right back."

He walked into the downstairs bathroom and wet a cloth in the fresh water they'd melted from the snow. He carried it back to the living room and held it in front of the fire to warm it up some. Then he gently wiped Nancy's face before handing it to Cayden to wash her up between her legs.

Taking care of her was important. He and Cayden would do their best to always take care of her. He took the cloth and dropped it into the basket in the back for laundry day. When he walked back through the kitchen, he stopped as he heard the two of them talking.

"Are you okay, Nancy?" Cayden asked.

"Yeah. Are you sure, Cayden?"

"I'm sure, honey. I just want you to be comfortable with this."

"I am. Mike's good to me and I loved what we did together," she said.

"Good. He's a good man and the two of us will always keep you safe." Cayden's voice broke. "I couldn't stand the idea that someone might take you from me."

"Seeing those scars on Mike really brought it home to me that we really do need him. Now, I'm attached to him. I don't want to lose him any more than I want to lose you, Cayden."

Mike sighed. They were good with what had happened. Some small part of him had worried it would all fall apart over the next few days, but hearing them talk about it with Nancy saying she was happy with their having made love gave him a sense of security about the three of them as a family.

He walked into the room and pulled on his pants. It was damn cold in the rest of the house. It had been a wonder his dick and balls hadn't shriveled up into nothing while he'd been standing in the kitchen door listening to them.

He watched Cayden help Nancy back into her clothes before he pulled on his own pants. Even disheveled as she was after their lovemaking, he thought she was beautiful. With her hair all tousled and her face flushed, she looked like heaven to him.

He reached over and pulled her to him for a kiss. He couldn't help but want to hold her and cuddle against her. He watched Cayden roll out the pallet in front of the fire. He hoped that the three of them would sleep there together tonight. He wanted to feel Nancy's body against his while they lay there. He'd been sleeping in the recliner while they'd shared the pallet each night. Tonight he wanted to share it with them. Share in their intimacy.

"I want a cup of tea before bed. What about you guys?" Nancy asked.

"Sounds good to me," Mike agreed.

Cayden nodded. "I'll get the tea. Mike, set the boiler over the fire, will you?"

Thirty minutes later they cuddled on the couch, sipping tea and talking about nothing much of anything. It warmed him even more than the hot tea did. He finally felt a part of something when he'd felt so empty and alone since his sister had moved in with her men. This was family.

* * * *

Nancy curled up on the couch while the two men were outside tending to the animals and moving more wood to the back porch. The front door was locked with a heavy chifforobe in front of the door for safety. They didn't use the front door so there was no reason to have it open in case someone wanted to break it down.

She had a roast cooking for dinner, but she wished she'd had something else to go with it. They were out of potatoes and carrots. There wasn't much left but meat to eat. She prayed spring was just around the corner like Mike had promised.

The back door slammed. She heard a grunt and the two men's voices in the kitchen. She grabbed a candle and walked into the other room to find Cayden sitting at the table with his foot propped up over one knee as Mike pulled off his boot.

"What's wrong? What happened?" she asked, hurrying over.

"The damn wood pile started rolling and got me on the leg and foot," he managed to squeeze out as he winced with the pain it caused for Mike to remove his boot.

"Is it broken?" she asked, holding the candle up.

"I don't know. Let's have a look." Mike rolled down the sock on Cayden's foot once he had the boot off.

Already the foot was red and swollen, as was his shin.

"Damn. It's swelling. I hope it's not broken." Cayden cursed.

"Hold on. I'm going to feel around on it." Mike began moving the foot and ankle with Cayden cursing as he did.

"I don't think it's broken. I think it's all soft tissue damage. You'll need to sit with it propped up and we'll pack snow around it to help with the swelling," Mike said.

"Fuck. I can't believe this," Cayden ground out.

"At least it's not broken, Cayden. It will be fine."

She watched as Mike helped Cayden limp into the other room and settled him on one of the recliners not too close to the fire so that the snow and ice they packed around his foot wouldn't melt too quickly.

"I'll chip out some ice from one of the buckets outside. We'll wrap it in a cloth then sit it over a plastic bin so that when it melts it won't get all over him," Mike told her.

They quickly set him up with the ice and listened to him complain and curse while they did. Nancy shook her head at him. She knew he was miserable and angry it had happened, but he really was being a little bit of a baby. Then again, she'd figured out a long time ago that men tended to be poor patients.

She bundled up and sat next to him off and on the rest of the evening, changing out his ice pack as it melted.

"That should be enough ice for the night," Mike finally told them. "You'll sleep better in front of the fire."

Mike helped her get him over to the pallet in front of the fire and lowered him to the ground. The three of them cuddled together under the blankets. Nancy had grown to enjoy this part of the night just before sleep when she had both men close to her. She'd usually end up curled over Cayden's side with Mike spooned behind her. Tonight was no different, except that she was worried she'd accidentally kick Cayden's bad leg.

"Relax, babe. He's okay," Mike whispered into her ear.

"I'm worried I'm going to hurt him in my sleep," she whispered back.

"I can hear you two so you might as well not whisper," Cayden said.

"You're not going to hurt him all that much if you accidentally kick him. He'll be fine."

"You're not the one with the sore leg, either," Cayden muttered.

Mike chuckled. "True, but we all need to sleep, and her worrying over it won't change a thing,"

"Mike's right, hon. I'm fine. If you hit it, you won't make it worse. Get some rest, Nancy." Cayden turned over, pulling her hand over his side as he did.

She worried until well into the night about Cayden's foot and leg. What if it had been broken? What would they have done? She had no clue how to set a broken anything. She was happy they were with Mike. He seemed to know what he was doing.

That thought reminded her of their lovemaking the night before. He'd been patient with her and hadn't tried to shove his cock down her throat. She hadn't known what to expect from him, but was relieved that he wasn't aggressive like some men tended to be. Though he and Cayden were as different as night and day, he'd been just as easy with her as Cayden when they'd had sex.

Finally, when she didn't think she'd ever fall asleep worrying about Cayden, she drifted off.

Chapter Twelve

"I know you guys aren't looking forward to all the work, but I can't wait to get outside and do something other than sit in front of the damn fireplace all day long." Nancy rubbed her hands together.

Mike had finally declared it time to start working on the garden. The snow had long since disappeared, turning the back yard into a mud puddle that had finally dried up enough for them to start working in it.

"It's going to take a good week to get the ground ready for planting. Don't wear yourself out, Nancy. Leave the work to us," Mike warned her.

"I can help. I'm not a weenie, Mike." Nancy propped her hands on her hips.

"I know, but there's no need for you to with the two of us working it," Mike said.

Cayden nodded. "You can rake up the clods we toss out into a pile."

She shrugged, planning to help any way she wanted to. In the end, they'd cave. They always did as long as it didn't have something to do with her health or safety. When one of those were in play, she lost every time.

All morning the men turned over the dirt in the garden, enlarging it to nearly twice the size Mike had originally had. She gathered the rocks and hard clods they threw out, tossing them out into the woods where Galahad chased after them each time. Then she went behind them with the hoe and cut up the turned ground behind them. It was hard work, something she hadn't done since they'd left the commune nearly a year ago. By the time they stopped for a break, her shoulders and arms felt as if she'd been pounding nails with a sledgehammer.

"You're overdoing it, babe," Mike said, giving her shoulders a light rub.

She winced. "I'm not doing much. It's good for me. I've gotten lazy sitting around all winter. I need the exercise."

"A little exercise is one thing, but you're pushing too hard. It's just the first day we've worked out here. Don't worry, there'll be plenty more ahead of us," Cayden told her.

She knew that was true, but she wanted to help. She needed to help. She wasn't one to sit back and let a man hand everything to her. Cayden knew her, so he didn't harp on her nearly as much as Mike did. That was okay, he'd learn.

The rest of the week went by in about the same way. They worked the garden until it was ready to plant. Mike said it would be ready the next day. They sat around the kitchen table that night going through the seeds they had and mapping out where they'd plant what. All of it was exciting to Nancy. She was going to enjoy this a lot more than she had back at the commune because it was all for them and they were doing all the work. Back there, it had been a community effort. She hadn't felt the same way.

"I'm beat. Ready for bed, guys?" Cayden asked.

"I'm going to wash up," Mike said.

Cayden and Nancy had already cleaned up. Mike had been the last one inside, having been the one to put away the garden tools.

Nancy spread out the pallet then stripped to climb under the covers. They'd decided to move upstairs to one of the beds there once they'd finished planting the garden and had the time to clean up the master bedroom.

She cuddled up as she waited on Cayden then Mike to join her. She was a little nervous inside. She planned to seduce them into taking her at the same time. They'd made love most nights, but it was always separately, and she wanted to feel them both inside of her at the same time. She needed that.

She wanted that.

By the time both men had joined her on the pallet, she was already a ball of need, reaching for Mike's cock with her hands. She stroked him until he was moaning in her ear.

"I want you, Mike. I want both of you inside of me," she said.

"Are you sure?" he asked.

"Honey, we have all the time in the world to get you ready. I don't want to hurt you," Cayden said.

"You won't. I'm ready. I need this, Cayden. I need to feel that we're all together as a family."

Mike kissed her, slipping his tongue inside to play and tempt hers. She loved how he kissed her. So different from Cayden's gentle exploring. Mike took and teased and tantalized her with how he explored her mouth. He didn't pull away until they were both breathless from the effort.

He ran his callused fingers over her breasts, kneading and squeezing them before teasing her nipples with his touch. He pulled and pinched them just right so that her pussy clenched at the need to be filled. Filled by him and Cayden.

Cayden slid two fingers into her hot, wet channel, pumping them in and out in a slow delicious rhythm that soon had her pushing back for more. He used his thumb to circle her clit then pinched it so that she moaned out loud. She was so damn ready for more.

"Climb on Mike, honey. Ride him for me, and I'll get you ready for my dick." Cayden urged her onto Mike's prone body.

She straddled him, letting her pussy glide over his engorged cock. The crown of him brushed enticingly over her clit with each slide of her pussy against him.

"Fuck, I'm so hard for you, babe. Lift up and let me see you take my dick inside that sweet pussy of yours."

Nancy lifted up as Mike fisted his hard shaft at the base and held it still so that she could slowly slide down the length of him until her pussy was flush against his groin. He filled her up and then some. Her inner walls stretched to accommodate his girth. Feeling him inside of her had her needing to move. She lifted up then allowed her body to sink back down again.

Mike held her hips and helped her lift and fall over and over. She felt Cayden behind her just before his hands caressed her ass cheeks. He rubbed them then spread them so that her back hole was exposed.

"Lean over him and let me get you ready, hon." Cayden's hot breath against her lower back felt wonderful.

Nancy relaxed against Mike's chest, turning her head so that she could hear his heart beat against her ear. It pounded out a rhythm much like hers. Then she was all about Cayden and what he was doing to her ass.

Something cool and greasy dripped down the crack of her ass. He rubbed it into her little rosette then added more. This time he pushed one finger into her back hole with the greasy liquid. He did this over and over until she was taking his entire finger, then two. The stretch didn't hurt. They'd played like this before, but she knew this time it would be different. She'd be taking Cayden's thick cock into her back channel. They'd never gone all the way before. She couldn't help but be a little nervous about it, but she was ready. Past ready. She needed her men as one.

"You okay, babe?" Mike asked as he stroked her head.

"I'm fine," she whispered back.

"She's ready," Cayden said. "Hold on."

The touch of Cayden's dick at her back hole had her stiffening up at first, but he stroked her ass.

"Relax, Nancy. Just breathe out and push out when I start to push in," Cayden said.

She breathed out and winced with the first press of Cayden's cock against her tight ring of muscles at her entrance. He pushed deeper until the crown of his dick popped through. A groan tore from her throat as he surged forward. It burned and pinched, but she breathed through it. Soon he was all the way inside of her, along with Mike. She felt full, overly full. She needed one of them to move. The need to push against both of them had her wiggling between them.

"I think she wants us to move," Mike said.

"Ya think?" Cayden's voice held a smile.

Mike pulled back, pressing her back against Cayden. Then Cayden pulled back, pushing her back onto Mike. They seesawed her between them in a slow rhythm that built the pressure growing inside of her at their double penetration of her body. She hadn't known it would be this way. She felt closer to them than she'd ever felt before. They were inside her. Branding her as their woman and she loved it.

The slight pain soon turned into a burning need for them to move faster, harder. She wanted them wild like she felt deep inside.

"More," she rasped out.

They took her at her word and began moving faster and deeper with each thrust. She'd never known that it could be like this. The sensations of pleasure were growing with each movement of her men inside of her. Her climax was going to kill her when it came. She could feel it so close that it seemed just out of reach.

"Not going to last," Mike ground out below her.

"I'm there. Too good," Cayden breathed out.

Nancy whimpered between them. She needed something more to get her there. She didn't know what, but she wanted to climax with them. As if knowing her dilemma, Mike reached between them and fingered her clit. It was enough and she screamed as the orgasm rushed over her, burning in her ass, and heating her from the inside out as she exploded between them.

She felt it when both men came as their seed coated her ass and her cunt in white-hot liquid that felt as if it went on and on. When she collapsed onto Mike, she felt Cayden's body at her back. Mike grunted when Cayden's weight pressed down on him.

"Move the hell over, man." Mike reached around Nancy to shove at Cayden.

"Sorry." Cayden gently pulled out of Nancy and rolled over to one side.

Both men's breathing was stuttering and loud. Nancy's own breath came in quiet gasps as she struggled. It had been everything she'd known it would be. She felt that unbreakable tether to both men now. They were truly together. She hugged Mike to her and reached over to grab Cayden's hand in hers.

He smiled at her. "Feel good, hon?"

"Perfect."

The last thing she noticed before she fell asleep was the two men cleaning her up and settling her between them.

* * * *

They worked on the garden all week, finally getting it ready to plant after five hard days of digging, hoeing, and raking out the clods. Nancy was one solid mass of soreness unlike anything she'd ever felt before. Back on the commune the women had only to deal with planting, weeding, and harvesting. The front work had been done by the men. She could now appreciate all their hard work.

"I'm beat," Cayden said once they'd rowed up the last part of the garden. "I'm not even sure I want to eat anything."

"I think my muscles are mush now," Nancy added.

"If we don't move around some tonight before we hit the bed we're going to be too stiff in the morning to get up," Mike reminded them.

"Uggg." Nancy made herself stand from where she'd been sitting on the ground.

Mike was right. The longer they sat there, the tighter their muscles would get. She shuffled toward the house, wondering what she could fix that would be easy and fast. She left the men outside to clean up the tools and put them away.

Thirty minutes later they gathered around the kitchen table and ate warmed up rabbit and gravy. She hoped they ended up with enough corn she would be able to make hoe cakes for some bread next fall and winter. It sucked not having bread. Grinding up the corn would be hard work, but it would be worth it.

"What are you thinking about over there?" Mike asked.

"Nothing, really. Just looking forward to harvest where we'll have fresh vegetables. I hope everything grows well."

"It's a long time until harvest, babe. Lots of work in between," he said.

"Remember all the work we had keeping the garden weeded last year before we left?" Cayden asked. "Now it's just us to water and weed."

"Don't remind me. Let me live in my fantasy world for a little longer," she muttered.

"Why don't you get ready for bed while we clean up the dishes? I know you're beat, babe." Mike stood, picking up the plates.

"You don't have to tell me twice." Nancy pushed herself up and strode from the kitchen.

They'd moved upstairs to the master bedroom the night before. She'd worked on cleaning it up and changing out the sheets to fresh ones. It gave them a little more room and certainly slept better than the pallet on the floor. As long as the weather was warm, they'd continue using the bed. Come winter, they'd be back in front of the fire.

After she'd cleaned up, Nancy climbed between the sheets and dozed off. Sometime later, she woke to both men loving on her body. Where had they found the strength? She giggled. Men never seemed too tired for sex.

"What's that for?" Mike asked.

"Nothing, just thinking that you two never get too tired for making love." Nancy groaned when Mike spread her legs and buried his face between them.

Cayden focused on her breasts, squeezing them then flicking her nipples before sucking one torrid peak into his hot, wet mouth. The feel of him sucking on them had her insides quivering.

Mike's tongue lapped at her folds. He spread them wide and licked up and down her slit until she was positive she'd go up in flames. When he teased her clit with the tip of his tongue Nancy groaned, thrashing her head from side to side. He was killing her with his wicked mouth. Between the two of them, she was sure she'd combust if they kept it up.

"You taste amazing, Nancy. I can't get enough of your sweet juices. I want to feel you come on my face, babe. Give it to me." Mike returned to sucking on her pussy lips then, out of the blue, he sucked hard on her clit.

Nancy screamed as she came. White hot flames seared her body as she gasped for breath while Mike continued licking her clit and Cayden sucked and pinched her nipples. She didn't think she'd ever come down and breathing became hit or miss for her.

Finally, they released the magical hold they'd had on her, allowing her to drift back into her body. She panted, not believing she'd ever be able to breathe right again.

"Damn, you look amazing when you come. You're lost in it when we get you there like that," Cayden said.

"We want you, babe. Think you can handle us after that?" Mike asked, his face showing nothing but male pride.

"Give me a second"—*pant, pant*—"to catch my breath," she said with ringing ears.

Mike ran his hand up and down her abdomen in a soothing motion. Cayden nuzzled her neck, kissing and sucking his way from her earlobe to her shoulder and back up again. It felt good having both men tend to her this way. She liked how they spoiled her and gave her the power over them when they made love depending on how she felt. Sure, they seduced her, but if she'd really felt too bad to have sex, they would have been fine with that. It made her love them all the more.

She stilled. Love? Did she really love both of them? When had it happened? How had it snuck up on her like this? She thought about it. Thought hard about it. Yes, she really did love them. Both of them.

That knowledge burned at her. She wanted to tell them but wasn't sure they'd feel the same way and that could be awkward. She'd wait for a while. Wait until she thought the time was right.

Mike kissed his way up her belly to her chest where he took her mouth with his, as Cayden sat back on his heels to wait his turn. She reveled in her new knowledge and kissed Mike back. They dueled with their tongues as he licked and sucked on hers. She nipped his lower lip then sucked it inside her mouth before he pulled back from the kiss to finger her pussy, making sure she was ready for him. How could she not be after the orgasm he'd given her?

When he fisted his hard cock and stroked it a few times while she watched, Nancy thought she'd die if he didn't hurry up and fuck her. She curled one leg around his ass and tried to pull him toward her.

"Easy, babe. I like seeing how your eyes go dark when you're lusting over my body. It really turns me on to know you want me as badly as I want you," Mike said.

"I do want you. Please, Mike. Don't make me wait."

He smiled then fit the crown of his dick at her opening and surged forward. She was wet enough that he was able to bury himself inside of her in one long thrust. The feel of him filling her pussy drew a gasp from her. She threw her head back and moaned as he pulled out and stroked back in over and over again.

"So good, baby. So fucking good." Mike held her hips as he pulled her against him with each thrust of his shaft inside her cunt.

The more he tunneled inside her, the higher she flew, knowing that when she reached the peak she'd break apart in his arms. She couldn't wait. Nancy dug her heels into his ass until he lifted her legs over his arms and bent over her as if he'd bury his cock so deep she'd taste him.

"Can't go much longer. Your cunt's milking me like a fucking cow, babe. So hot and wet and tight. I can't last."

Cayden reached over and began tugging and pinching her nipples until she exploded, her climax carrying Mike over with her. She felt hot spurts of his seed coat her insides as the roaring in her head drowned out whatever he shouted as he came with her.

Long seconds later, Nancy panted and gasped with Mike lying on top of her. She smiled at how he seemed to be having just as much trouble breathing as she did. Two orgasms in one night was nothing for her with her men loving her like they did. If Cayden had anything to say about it, it would be three. She sighed. She loved her men. It still thrilled her to realize that.

"Move over, Mike. Let her catch her breath." Cayden shoved at the other man.

Mike grunted and slid off her to one side. He rested his hand on her belly and kissed her neck.

"Love you, babe."

Nancy stilled. Had he meant it or was that just the afterglow talking? Did men even have that? She wanted to tell them both she loved them, but was it really the right time?

"I love you, too, hon. You're the best thing that's ever happened to me." Cayden threaded his fingers with hers.

She sighed. This felt right. Perfect.

"I love both of you. I just realized how much tonight. You're the best men a woman could ever have," she admitted.

"You really love me?" Mike asked, propping himself up on one hand.

"Yes. I do. I guess it snuck up on me, but I do love you, just like I love Cayden." She smiled up at him.

The relief that flowed over his features told Nancy that she'd been right to tell him now. He bent over and kissed her soft and sweet on the lips before kissing her forehead, as well.

"I'll make sure you have the best of everything I can give you, babe. You mean that much to me. We'll get solar panels up so that you can have a hot bath every night and I'll introduce you to my sister. She's going to love you," Mike said.

"I can't wait."

"Feel like another round of scorching hot sex?" Cayden asked, giving her a devilish smile.

"Are you offering?" she teased.

"I'm promising it'll be wild, hon."

"Then yes, do your dirtiest, Cayden."

He chuckled and kissed her before having her turn over on her hands and knees. She giggled as she lifted her ass in the air. He slapped each ass cheek then bent over and nipped at them, as well.

"I can't wait to feel just how good you'll feel to my dick, hon. You're going to burn me alive, aren't you."

Nancy wiggled her butt as she looked over her shoulder at him. "Are you going to talk or fuck me?"

He grinned then fit his cock to her slit and thrust inside of her. She closed her eyes and enjoyed the way his thick dick parted her tender tissue. She was a little touchy from Mike's fucking earlier, but not too sore to take Cayden's loving.

"Oh, hell, Nancy. You're squeezing me like a warm wet velvet lined glove. So damn good," Cayden rasped out.

"More, Cayden. Fuck me harder."

She wanted everything he had to give her. She loved when they lost control and thrust inside of her as if they were trying to get all the way inside her. She wanted it all. She wanted their seed and their love. She wanted to give them happy days, hot sultry nights, and a child to love. Maybe not this soon, but soon. Nancy wanted it all with them. Every second, every minute, and every hour that she could get.

Cayden pounded into her, using his hands on her hips to pull her back against him as he surged deep inside of her. She dug her hands into the sheets to keep from banging her head against the headboard. Then Mike was there, placing his body between her and it. She loved that he thought about her like that and wanted to protect her.

Nancy gasped as Cayden adjusted his position so that his cock rubbed over that sensitive place inside her. Soon, she was moaning in pleasure, knowing she was going to come again. The feel of his shaft and the head of it stroking over that one place inside her that guaranteed she'd climax had her burying her face in the sheets as she came, yelling it into the covers.

"Holy hell, woman. You're going to strangle me," Cayden said. Then let out a roar as he ground into her from behind.

She felt as if her orgasm had turned her inside out. She collapsed so that the only thing holding her up at all was Cayden's cock deep inside of her. She groaned when he slowly withdrew and plopped down on the bed next to her. He had one hand over his eyes as he gasped and panted along with her.

"I'll be right back, babe. Gonna get a washcloth for you." Mike climbed out of bed and shuffled into the bathroom. A few seconds later he returned with a wet cloth. "It's going to be cold, but you'll feel better if you're not so sticky down there."

He was right. She yelped when he started cleaning her girly parts. If it were possible, her pussy would have shivered at the cold touch but he was right. She'd feel better if she were cleaned up.

"Thanks, Mike."

"Go to sleep, babe. We've got a long day ahead of us tomorrow."

"I love you, Mike."

"I love you, too, Nancy. More than you'll ever know."

"Love you, Cayden."

"Love you more, hon."

Only Nancy knew that wasn't possible. She loved her men equally and more than life itself. She hadn't realized it was possible to love two men at the same time, but now she knew it. They were hers.

THE END

WWW.MARLAMONROE.COM

Siren Publishing, Inc.
www.SirenPublishing.com

Lightning Source UK Ltd.
Milton Keynes UK
UKHW011014051118
331793UK00013B/1442/P